APR 0 3 2010

BY:

LILY DALE
DISCOVERING

ALSO BY WENDY CORSI STAUB

Lily Dale: Awakening

Lily Dale: Believing

Lily Dale: Connecting

LILY DALE
DISCOVERING

Wendy Corsi Staub

Walker & Company ✺ New York

First published in the United States of America in 2009 by
Walker Publishing Company, Inc.
Visit Walker & Company's Web site at www.bloomsburyteens.com

For information about permission to reproduce selections from
this book, write to Permissions, Walker & Company,
175 Fifth Avenue, New York, New York 10010

Library of Congress Cataloging-in-Publication Data
Staub, Wendy Corsi.
Lily Dale : discovering / by Wendy Corsi Staub.
        p.   cm.
Summary: After almost being killed while trying to discover how
her mother died, Calla tries desperately to use both her psychic powers
and investigative skills to learn the truth about her mother's life,
and to find out what these secrets may mean for her.
ISBN-13: 978-0-8027-9786-5 • ISBN-10: 0-8027-9786-5
[1. Psychic ability—Fiction. 2. Psychics—Fiction. 3. Grandmothers—Fiction.
4. Mothers—Fiction. 5. Lily Dale (N.Y.)—Fiction.
6. Mystery and detective stories.] I. Title. II. Title: Discovering.
PZ7.S804Lm 2009   [Fic]—dc22   2008044674

Typeset by Westchester Book Composition
Printed in the U.S.A. by Quebecor World Fairfield
2 4 6 8 10 9 7 5 3 1

All papers used by Walker & Company are natural, recyclable products
made from wood grown in well-managed forests. The manufacturing processes
conform to the environmental regulations of the country of origin.

For the sweetest June rose: my new niece,
Gianna Marie Corsi

And for my guys: Morgan, Brody, and Mark

LILY DALE

DISCOVERING

PROLOGUE

New York City
Monday, October 8
1:46 p.m.

If you look hard enough, you can always find it.

The wise man who once said that to Laura wasn't talking about the Internet, but the phrase has become her mantra for all things.

He was right, of course.

There it is.

She's been looking, and she's found it.

Her hand trembling on the mouse, she leans closer to the monitor and clicks to enlarge the window.

LOCAL WOMAN ARRESTED IN FLORIDA

Local woman.

Sharon Logan.

Whenever Laura has a chance to get to a computer, she enters the name in a search engine and prays nothing will come up.

Today, her prayers went unanswered.

According to the online news account from her hometown paper, Sharon Logan is being held without bail in Tampa for attacking a girl named Calla Delaney and trying to drown her in her family's swimming pool. She's also being questioned about the murder last summer of the girl's mother, Stephanie Delaney, originally ruled an accidental fall down the stairs.

Those poor people.

Jaw set grimly, hand unsteady on the mouse button, Laura closes out the screen. That's all she needs to know.

It was only a matter of time before something like this happened.

That's why she had to get away. She just couldn't take it anymore—the constant tension, the growing paranoia, the constant, smothering attention; being treated as if she were still a child, even now that she's in her twenties.

Laura knew that if she stayed, eventually something would have to give. She didn't want to be there to witness it.

But . . . murder.

She never really imagined it would be that extreme.

And . . . Florida?

What was she doing in Florida?

Who are the Delaneys?

Does it matter?

Maybe it should.

But after all those years of being the girl who lived in the purple house with the crazy lady, all Laura cares about is that she's finally free.

Free, and not looking back.

"Excuse me, miss . . . are you done with that computer? Because we have people waiting to use it."

She looks up to see a librarian. Not one of the friendly ones she's gotten to know since she started coming here a few months ago; rather, the one who shushes people and scowls a lot when they hog the computers.

"Oh . . . sorry. I'm finished."

She grabs her backpack, makes her way through the hushed library, and emerges on a crowded Manhattan street.

People rush past without giving her a second glance. No one knows who she is. Or who Sharon Logan is. No one cares.

That's why she's here. That's just the way she wants it.

Especially now that Laura knows it finally happened. The crazy lady finally snapped.

Murder.

Laura knew, when she woke up this morning, that today would be the day the search engine would yield something.

If you look hard enough, you can find it.

Years ago, when he said those words, he was talking about hope.

About finding hope, in the midst of despair.

"If you look hard enough, Laura," he said, handing her tissue after tissue to dry her tears, "you can find it."

She clung to those words, somehow managed to find a glimmer of light on the darkest days; just a shred of hope to keep her going.

Yet now that it's all over—now that she's here, and Sharon Logan is a thousand miles away, in jail for murder . . .

Now, ironically, Laura's mantra has been altered.

Every morning, she wakes up thinking it, praying it:

If you really, really, *really* want to get lost—really *need* to get lost—then no one can ever find you.

ONE

Lily Dale, New York
Monday, October 8
1:46 p.m.

"All right. Tell me everything. And I mean everything!"

Calla Delaney and her father look at each other, then back at Odelia Lauder, standing in the front hall waiting impatiently for one of them to start talking.

"Gammy, it's really complicated." Calla sets down her heavy duffel bag and shifts the laptop computer bag to her other shoulder, wishing her grandmother hadn't pounced on her and Dad the second they walked in the door from the airport.

It's been a long day already, saying good-bye to the Wilsons down in Florida, driving to the airport in Tampa, flying from there to New York City, then from New York to Buffalo, waiting for the luggage, renting a car, then driving almost an hour south to reach Lily Dale.

Odelia's little two-story cottage with its peeling pinkish orange paint was a welcome sight. They arrived just as a cold rain began falling from an overcast sky, typical weather here in southwestern New York State.

Calla, in jeans and a fleece sweatshirt, was prepared for it.

Dad, wearing shorts, flip-flops, and a T-shirt, was not.

"I'll get some warmer clothes when we get there," he told Calla earlier when she warned him that his outfit, which is fine for Florida—or Southern California, where he's been on a teaching sabbatical since August—just won't cut it up here.

Poor Dad. It's not like he even had a chance to pack a bag for what's turning out to be an extended, unexpected trip east. He hopped on a plane from LA on Saturday when the Tampa police informed him that his daughter had just been attacked by a lunatic killer.

Again.

Only Dad doesn't know about the first time, well over a month ago.

That, of course, was a different lunatic killer.

Right.

Incredible, really, the things that have happened to Calla since she came to live with her grandmother in this tiny, gated lakeside village filled with century-old gingerbread cottages . . . and psychic mediums.

"Odelia," Dad says, "there's a lot to discuss."

"I'm listening." Gammy looks from him to Calla to him to Calla. "Hello?"

Not knowing where to begin, Calla avoids her grandmother's expectant gaze. She stoops to pick up Gert, who's rubbing against her ankles, purring, welcoming her back.

"Why don't we let Calla go up to her room and relax," Dad suggests, "and I'll fill you in."

"That's a great idea. Calla, why don't you—"

"No!" She protests so loudly that poor Gert leaps from her arms and flees up the steps past Miriam, who's materialized about halfway up, keeping a ghostly eye on things.

Both Dad and Odelia gape at Calla, who scowls back at them. "Please don't shuttle me off to my room like a little girl. I'm not. I'm almost eighteen." Well, she *will* be, in another six months. "I can deal with what happened. I mean, it happened to *me*, remember? Maybe I want to talk about it. Maybe I *need* to."

She does?

You do?

Hmm. The protest sort of popped out of her.

Who knows? Her head has been spinning since the plane touched down. Maybe she does need to get everything out into the open.

Then again, just a few moments ago, the last thing she wanted to do was rehash the events of the past few days.

Face it. You really don't know what you want.

"Oh, sweetie, you've been through so much. It just breaks my heart." Her grandmother throws a pair of strong maternal arms around her.

Suddenly, for all her longing to be seen as an adult, Calla feels as though she's about to crumple and cry like a baby.

"I'm okay," she manages to squeak out unconvincingly.

No, she isn't. She *used to* be okay. Before everything—before she lost her mother. Before her life fell apart.

She used to be sweet and accommodating and happy and normal.

"You can't possibly be okay. And you don't have to be. Not yet. But you *will* be," Odelia promises, reaching out to brush strands of Calla's long brown hair back from her face.

Then, for the first time, she seems to notice the laptop bag. "What is that?"

"Mom's computer. Now I'll be able to check my e-mail and do research for homework right from here, Gammy."

Among other things.

"But this house isn't wired for the Internet, sweetie."

"That's okay. All I need is a phone jack. I can do a dial-up connection."

"Well, then, you're in luck. We have a few of those. In fact, there's one right in your bedroom."

"Really?" She'd never noticed it before.

Odelia nods. "Your mother begged me for her own phone when she hit twelve or thirteen. Back then, we didn't have cordless, and she wanted privacy to talk to her friends. She used to be on it forever."

Calla finds it hard to imagine her hyperefficient mother lounging around chatting on the phone for hours. Mom wasn't big on leisurely conversation—telephone or otherwise. She liked to get right to the point and then move on. In both business situations and in personal ones.

"Let's go into the kitchen," Odelia suggests. "I made lunch. You haven't eaten yet, have you, Jeff?"

"We grabbed a couple of bran muffins at the airport earlier this morning, but Calla barely touched hers."

"Well, they probably didn't put the Raisinets in, like I do when I make them."

"What?" Dad's eyes are wide.

"Didn't you ever hear of raisins in bran muffins?"

"Raisins, yes. Raisinets, no."

"Well, chocolate is good in anything," Odelia tells Dad with a shrug, eyes gleaming behind the pink plastic cat's-eye frames of her glasses—which, of course, clash violently with her frizzy dyed red hair and her purple sweater.

If Calla were in a chatty mood, she might bring up the "snicker-noodles" her grandmother served for dinner one night—with cut-up Snickers bars as a featured ingredient.

Was that only a few weeks ago? It seems like a year, at least, has passed since that night.

And it seems even longer since Calla's had any kind of appetite.

"Who am I to question your recipes, Odelia? You've always been a great cook." Dad sniffs the air. "Something smells good. Tuna melts?"

Calla doubts that. Tuna melts would be far too ordinary for a creative chef like Odelia.

"No, but you're close," she tells Dad. "Come see."

Calla smells tuna, too. Tuna . . . and a faint hint of lilies of the valley.

That can mean only one thing.

Aiyana is here.

She takes a quick look around the room for her Native

American spirit guide, whose presence is always accompanied by the scent of Mom's favorite flower.

No sign of Aiyana, but . . .

Calla sniffs again. Yes, the floral smell is real, and of course there's not a blossom in sight. Fragrant lilies of the valley only bloom in springtime.

Aiyana . . . where are you?

Calla wonders if she's just too worn out today to connect with the spirit. She's still new to this—she needs more practice when it comes to tuning in to the energy.

Tuning out, as well. Sometimes she finds herself bombarded with images and voices. It can be frightening.

Her grandmother promised she'd get the hang of it, though. That's why she enrolled Calla in a Beginning Mediumship course with classes every Saturday morning.

Aiyana, are you trying to tell me something?

"Calla? Are you okay?"

She turns to see Odelia watching her with concern.

"I'm . . . fine. Just a little spacey, I guess. Maybe I need to go upstairs and lie down." *And see if Aiyana comes to me there.*

"You need to eat first. Come on." Keeping one fleshy arm draped around Calla's shoulders, her fingers resting on the strap of the bag that contains Mom's computer, Odelia leads the way through small rooms cluttered with mismatched furniture, books and knickknacks, threadbare carpets, and outdated kitchen appliances.

Funny . . . the ramshackle Victorian cottage is a far cry from the upscale, three-thousand-square-foot house where Calla grew up, but this feels much more like home to her now.

Maybe because the Tampa house is where Mom died.

10

This is where Mom lived—until she was about Calla's age, anyway.

Then Stephanie Lauder left, and she never came back. Never, it seems, even looked back.

She didn't like to talk about her childhood. Calla always assumed that was because she was a child of divorce—her father left when she was young. Or maybe it was because Mom didn't get along very well with Odelia. Or because she just wasn't big on nostalgia.

Whatever. You'd think Mom might have mentioned to Calla or Dad that her hometown happened to be populated by psychic mediums—and that her own mother, Odelia, was one of them.

Calla didn't find out about any of that until she came to visit her grandmother after Mom's death.

No, not *death*.

Now they all know her fatal fall down the stairs wasn't an accident.

It was murder. She was murdered.

That's not all.

Mom had a deep, dark secret—one Calla stumbled upon a few days ago, when she was snooping through her mother's e-mail files looking for clues to her death. The secret remains locked in Mom's laptop, protected by a password Calla managed to figure out—perhaps with a little help from her sixth sense.

She didn't tell a soul about what she'd discovered. Not Dad, not the police. It was too shocking, too personal, too . . . painful.

Even now, whenever Calla allows herself to think about what she learned, she's swept by an overwhelming sense of

11

betrayal by the mother she thought she had known—the mother who now feels like a stranger to her.

How could Mom have kept such an important secret for all these years? Why?

The whole truth, Calla is sure, lies in her mother's e-mail files. But she couldn't bring herself to go on reading them that day in Florida.

No, she only got as far as to learn the shocking truth: that Mom and her high school boyfriend, Darrin Yates—both of whom were murdered in the last few months—had, over twenty years ago, had a child together.

Which means somewhere out there, Calla must have a half sibling.

TWO

Odelia bustles over to take a casserole dish out of the oven. "You're going to love this, Jeff. It'll warm your soul."

"I take it you're thinking my soul needs warming?"

"I'm thinking, whose doesn't? And it's one of my specialties."

"Soul warming?"

"Rice ring!"

"Rice ring," Dad echoes, nodding. "What is it, though?"

"It's just what it sounds like . . . see?" Odelia drops a crocheted pot holder onto the table and plops the oval dish on top of it.

Calla peers at the contents. Yup. That's a ring of rice, all right. Mounds of steaming white rice, mixed with peas, line the perimeter of the dish. Pooled in the center basin is something creamy and lumpy with greenish gray flecks.

It doesn't look particularly appetizing, but it does smell

pretty good. Which is the case with many of her grand-mother's specialties.

"What else is in there?" Dad eyes it somewhat suspiciously. "Besides a ring of rice, I mean."

"Peas."

"Yup, see the peas. A whole lot of peas."

Dad hates peas.

He's not all that crazy about rice, either, Calla remembers. Not the brown rice Mom used to make, anyway. She was really into healthy food. Unlike Gammy.

Funny how Mom and Gammy really were opposites.

Kind of like Mom and me.

"It's just tuna fish and cream of celery soup, and stop mak-ing faces at my rice ring, Jeff." Gammy swats Dad's arm with the other pot holder.

Mom made that, Calla realizes.

Yes, her mother made that pot holder and the matching one beneath the casserole dish. She was a little girl, and she used one of those plastic loom kits; she got it for Christmas.

Calla closes her eyes.

There's Mom, about ten years old, curled up in a chair beside a tinsel-covered tree, weaving loops of colored fabric as snow swirls beyond the window.

It's not her imagination. No, this scene—like so many other images that have flashed into her head over the years—really happened.

It's a psychic vision.

She's been having them all her life. She just never knew exactly what they were until she moved in with Odelia, in a strange little town populated almost entirely by spiritualists.

14

This is where Calla first started seeing dead people, too. Well, not just *here*.

Lately, they're everywhere. Or maybe they always have been, but Calla never realized it, or knew how—or where—to look for them.

She opens her eyes and glances around her grandmother's kitchen, making it a point to tune in.

Still no sign of Aiyana. And no longer a telltale whiff of lilies of the valley.

But she does spot Miriam—the resident ghost, whose husband built the house well over a century ago—hovering in the corner by the fridge, watching Odelia dish up the casserole.

She's definitely not the only spirit hanging around this house. And Calla's ability to see her is about as much a novelty around Lily Dale as the rain is.

It all goes with the local territory. Psychic impressions, apparitions, premonitions, too. She's had those all her life— has always known things she had no way of knowing.

The first few times it happened, when she was really little, she told her mother. Mom seemed uneasy and made her promise not to tell anybody, so Calla didn't.

Not until she got to Lily Dale, where everyone and their brother has premonitions.

No wonder Mom had to leave. She was always much too practical for stuff like that. Unlike the rest of the world—or so it seemed to Calla—she didn't believe in Santa Claus, or even in God. So why would she believe in ghosts?

It must have been hard for her to live in the Dale and not be a part of things. To be one of the few "mere mortals" here—as Calla's new friend Evangeline jokingly calls outsiders.

Calla—who stepped into those shoes when she arrived back in August—shed them pretty quickly.

It wasn't that she was eager to be like everyone else here. In fact, it was exactly opposite.

But she had no choice. She discovered that she *was* one of them.

Now there's a new outsider in the Dale. One who isn't nearly as likely to find that he belongs here.

"How about a cup of coffee, Jeff?" Gammy asks as he raises a forkful of rice, then stifles a yawn.

"That would be great. I could use some caffeine."

"I'll make a pot. Calla? Do you want some? You look a little droopy, too."

"She doesn't drink coffee."

Okay, true. But Calla wishes her father didn't find it necessary to answer for her.

Is this how it's going to be from now on? Dad here, in her space, putting words into her mouth, imposing all sorts of rules . . .

"I'd love a cup, Gammy. Thank you."

"You're drinking coffee now?" Dad looks totally dismayed.

Instant guilt.

"Just sometimes," Calla murmurs.

More like *once*, on a date with Blue Slayton, the cute guy she was trying to impress back when she first got here.

Still, she's almost eighteen. She can drink coffee if she wants to . . . can't she? Gammy offers it to her all the time. And it's not like it's a cigarette or a shot of whiskey or drugs.

"Caffeine is a drug," Dad says, as if he's read her mind.

Only—being a mere mortal—of course, he didn't.

16

"It's not good for you, you know."

"Dad, you can't go around treating me like a little girl."

"Sure I can," he says easily, around a mouthful of rice. "You know, Odelia, this is pretty good."

"Of course it is." She pours water into the coffeemaker. "I'm a great cook."

"Modest, too."

Odelia cracks a smile, presses a button, and returns to the table.

"Okay," she says, sitting down. "I'm ready. Tell me everything. First things first, though, Jeff—like I told you on the phone yesterday, you're welcome to take my room until you find a place of your own around here—"

"Odelia, like I said, I can't put you out of your bed. The couch will be—"

"Wait, Jeff, let me finish. You don't have to put me out of my bed or sleep on the couch. You've met Ramona Taggart next door—well, she has a spare bedroom, and she says it's all yours, for as long as you want it."

"Really." Dad looks pleased.

He's met Odelia's flaky—and beautiful—neighbor a few times when he visited, and Calla definitely sensed sparks flying between the two of them.

Which shocked her. Not just because she can't imagine her father with a woman who isn't her mother, but because she can't imagine her father with a woman like Ramona.

Then again . . . he was married to Mom. A straight-shooting, pragmatic, workaholic businesswoman, she, too, was drastically different from Dad. And from Ramona.

I guess opposites really do attract.

Calla can't help but think of Jacy Bly. He's not her opposite—more like a kindred spirit—but they're definitely attracted.

Like her, Jacy is a relative newcomer to Lily Dale, uprooted from his home on a Native American reservation down on the southern tier. Like her, he moved into a house with a medium's shingle out front and found himself in the care of strangers— loving strangers, but strangers, nonetheless. Like her, he eventually found himself at home here in the Dale.

Perhaps most important, Jacy is—like Calla—a gifted medium in his own right.

"Listen, it's not a fancy guest suite, by any means," Gammy is telling Dad. "It's just big enough for a twin bed and a dresser—but it's a bed, not a couch, and you'll have room to store your things. In this house, there's not even room to store *my* things, and Calla's."

And Mom's, Calla adds silently. Her grandmother hasn't thrown away any of her late daughter's childhood possessions. For Calla, this house has been a welcome shrine to her mother's past, a soothing balm for her own grief.

"Since I pretty much just have the clothes on my back, and some stuff I grabbed from the house down in Florida, storage space isn't a big issue for me right now, Odelia. But the room sounds great," Dad adds hastily—maybe too hastily, because he glances from Gammy to Calla, saying, like he's still reluctant to accept the invitation, "I just hate to put anybody out. . . ."

"Oh, you're not putting Ramona out, Jeff. She kept telling me to make sure you knew that she'd really love to have you."

Of course she would.

"Plus," Odelia continues, "you'll be right next door to Calla. What could be better? Right, Calla?"

She's got to be kidding.

What could be better than to have Dad move into a house that bears the shingle RAMONA TAGGART, REGISTERED MEDIUM?

Talk about baptism by fire.

Dad has visited Calla in Lily Dale a couple of times, but he still has no idea what goes on around here.

Sure, he's driven past the sign at the wrought-iron gate: LILY DALE ASSEMBLY . . . WORLD'S LARGEST CENTER FOR THE RELIGION OF SPIRITUALISM. And, yes, he knows that the lakeside community was the birthplace of modern spiritualism back in the eighteen hundreds. He's also well aware that some of Odelia's neighbors do psychic readings, thanks to the hand-painted shingles in front of their homes.

Like REV. DORIS HENDERSON, CLAIRVOYANT.

And ANDY BRIGHTON, PSYCHIC MEDIUM.

"New Age freaks," Dad called them, and asked if they hold seances and read crystal balls.

Calla enlightened him just enough to take the edge off but figured that if he knew the whole truth, he'd yank her right out of Lily Dale.

At first, she was desperate to stay and delve into her mother's past, thinking she'd find the key to the mystery surrounding Mom's death. But as time went on, she felt more and more connected to her grandmother, and her new friends—and to the place itself. She decided to spend her senior year at Lily Dale High, rather than in California with Dad. Yes, she's missed him, but in a way, it's also been a relief to have some distance between them, considering all that's been going on here.

So much for space. Now that Dad's decided to move into Ramona's house, he's about to discover that he's a mere mortal living among the dead—and among the living who can communicate with the dead.

He's not going to appreciate that any more than Calla did when she first got here.

But it's not like he's eventually likely to discover—as she did—that he, too, can see dead people.

While the spiritualists here believe that anyone is capable of connecting with spirits, that it's a skill that can be developed like any other, they also believe that it comes much more readily to certain people, who inherit it from their parents and grandparents like any other hereditary trait.

Calla, as the granddaughter of one of Lily Dale's most powerful mediums, is genetically predisposed through her mother's side of the family. And it's a talent that seems to have skipped a generation, because Mom didn't have a psychic bone in her body.

"So now that we've settled where you'll be staying, Jeff, why don't you tell me exactly what happened in Florida?"

Dad puts down his fork. "I really did cover most of it on the phone, Odelia."

"An insane woman—who, for God knows what reason, snuck into your house a few months ago and pushed Stephanie down the stairs—came back and tried to kill Calla, too. That's what I know."

"That's exactly what happened." Dad pushes his plate away, suddenly looking ill.

Calla sets down her fork and shudders, remembering the crazed look in Sharon Logan's eyes.

"But who *is* this person?" Gammy asks. "She's from this area, didn't you say?"

"Not here—about a hundred miles away, I guess. Geneseo."

"I can't imagine the connection. Stephanie never even set foot in Geneseo, as far as I know. Not when she lived here, anyway."

"I don't know about that, but . . . Calla's been there. Calla's met the woman."

"What?!"

Great. Did he have to bring that up now?

Calla shifts her weight uncomfortably in her chair and tries not to look at her grandmother.

She had confessed that part of the story when they were at the police station yesterday. But only because the detective asked her directly, in front of her father, whether she had ever seen the woman before.

How could she lie?

She admitted that she'd been to Geneseo and had briefly met Sharon there. She just didn't tell the police—or Dad—the entire story.

But that's not lying. It's just omitting. There's a big difference.

If Calla admitted that she'd been led to Sharon Logan while searching for Mom's missing high school boyfriend, Darrin, she might somehow be forced to admit the rest of the truth: not just that Mom and Darrin had had a baby all those years ago . . .

But that they were, according to Mom's e-mail, apparently having an affair for months before they were both killed.

The knowledge is hard enough for Calla to swallow. It

would be much too painful for Dad to hear after all he's been through.

"When did you meet her, Calla?" Gammy demands, with an ominous look in her eye.

"Last weekend, when I went to Geneseo." She might as well confess as much as she can, with Dad sitting right here. "Remember when I said I was going to the homecoming dance with Jacy? I really went there."

"To Geneseo. So you lied to me."

Calla nods miserably. "I'm sorry."

"And Jacy—what? Covered for you? Went with you?"

"He went with me. He drove me, actually."

At least Gammy doesn't scold her for the lie. She probably will at some point, but right now, she seems interested only in getting answers.

"Why did you go there?"

"Because . . ." Calla flicks a glance at her father, who is listening intently, of course. "See, a couple of weeks ago, Evangeline and I had gone to this psychic reading here in the Dale . . . with Patsy. You know Patsy?"

Gammy glances at Dad, then nods. "I know Patsy," is all she says, obviously getting it.

Patsy Metcalf is a friend of hers—who also happens to be the instructor of Calla's Beginning Mediumship class.

Which, naturally, Dad doesn't know Calla is taking.

He was disapproving enough when she told him—and the two police detectives, Lutz and Kearney—that she'd been led to Sharon Logan through a psychic reading in the first place.

"Calla, why would you waste your time on that kind of thing?" Dad had asked at the time.

"It wasn't a waste, Dad. There was obviously something to it, right?"

He muttered something about—what else?—New Age freaks.

But when he saw how seriously the police were taking her, he closed his mouth and didn't say another word about it.

The detectives took down contact information for Patsy and wanted to know about Bob, her fellow student, who'd had the vision. Something tells Calla that Lutz and Kearney might be paying a visit to Lily Dale in the near future.

Now, she explains to her grandmother as vaguely as possible how a psychic vision—not her own—of a purple house in Geneseo had led her to Sharon Logan's doorstep.

"I just don't understand what you were looking for, though," Dad says.

I was looking for Darrin. The guy Mom was with when she was supposedly away on all those business trips.

But she can't tell her father about that.

"I wanted answers about Mom's death, Dad. But Jacy and I barely talked to her. She wasn't very friendly, to say the least."

"Did she threaten you?"

"No. It wasn't like that. She just told us to go away."

That happened right *after* Calla and Jacy showed Sharon Logan a photo of Mom and Darrin.

"And this woman killed my daughter." Odelia swallows hard, and her hands clench into fists on the table.

"She hadn't confessed when we left Florida," Dad tells

her. "She's not talking at all, as far as I know. The police said they'll let me know what she says when she cracks."

Calla voices the question that's been on her mind since the arrest. "What if she doesn't crack and confess?"

"Then I guess we'll never know the truth about what happened to your mother."

Calla knows what happened, though. She's seen it.

She's had visions, horrible visions, of Sharon Logan pushing Mom down the stairs, wearing a signet ring that bore the Logan family crest. That's all the proof she needs.

She knows, too, that Sharon killed Darrin. His murder, in Portland, Maine, a few weeks before Mom's, remains officially unsolved.

Nobody could possibly link Darrin to Mom. As far as she can tell, neither her father nor the Florida police have any idea he even existed.

He died under an assumed name, Tom Leolyn, having been missing from Lily Dale for almost twenty years. He contacted Mom this past Valentine's Day, wanting to see her. She snuck away to meet him in Boston, where, apparently, he dropped a bombshell on her.

Something about their child, and something he did for which he wanted her forgiveness.

That was as far as Calla could bring herself to read back in Florida.

Dad and the police don't know about the e-mails.

Maybe they should be told. Maybe Calla should forget about protecting Dad, or figuring things out on her own. Maybe she should just spill the whole story.

But what would she gain from that?

Nobody knows why Sharon Logan did what she did, but maybe it really was random. Anyway, she's in custody. She can't hurt anyone now.

And if Calla tells what she knows, Mom's secret baby and affair would be dragged out into the open.

Calla looks at her father.

He's wearing a faraway expression, eyes glistening with tears.

He's thinking about Mom.

I can't let him find out that she was in love with another man, sneaking around to be with him. That would kill him.

Now that he's here in Lily Dale, can she bring herself to find out what really happened between her mother and Darrin? What if the truth comes out, anyway? Then Dad will have to live forever with the knowledge that his wife had a baby with another man, hid it from him, and then cheated on him.

How could you, Mom? How could you do this to him? To us?

THREE

"How about that coffee now, Jeff?" Gammy asks, pushing her chair back from the table.

"Sure. Thanks."

"And you need something sweet to go with it."

"You know me, Odelia."

She *does* know him. Somehow Calla is surprised to hear her grandmother acknowledge Dad's little quirk: that he always likes to have a cookie or sweet roll with his coffee.

But then, Dad was Odelia's son-in-law long before he was Calla's father. She probably knew him well, way back when. She used to visit them a lot in the old days, before the rift.

"You know, Jeff," Gammy bustles over to the counter, "you look light years younger without that gray beard. I'm glad you finally shaved it off."

"It wasn't *all* gray."

"Mostly gray."

"Well . . . yeah."

"What made you decide to get rid of it? You've had it forever."

"Not forever. Only since the third grade." Dad winks at Calla across the table as Odelia chuckles.

He *does* look light years younger, Calla notices. His black hair is still slightly shaggy, but it actually has some shape to it now, thanks to some fancy LA barber.

He's also exchanged his wire-rimmed glasses for contact lenses, bringing out his dark brown eyes. His T-shirts haven't been as ratty as usual, either.

It's so ironic. Mom would have been pleased to see him spruced up. She was always nagging him about the way he looked.

Now that she's gone, he's grooming himself and dressing the way she wished he would have.

Calla can't help but wonder whether it's just a sad coincidence . . . or whether the way he looks now has something to do with Mom being gone.

Maybe he's dating again already.

Or maybe he just wants to.

She can't help but think again of Ramona.

"You know, I never really spent much time worrying about stuff like that," he says, mostly to her grandmother. "You know . . . the gray beard. It was just there. Like everything else. But lately, I've had a lot of time to think about things, the way they've been, and decided to try to change whatever needs changing."

"Like shaving." Gammy shoots a glance in Calla's direction.

So does Dad. "Like a lot of things."

"Well, I'm really going to like having you around for a while, Jeff. We haven't spent much time together since . . . Florida."

Florida. Gammy means the funeral. She flew down, of course, and stayed with them. Before that, Calla hadn't seen her in years.

That's the other thing. . . .

The argument that's been haunting Calla since she arrived here, in a recurring dream. The scene is always the same: her mother and grandmother are emotional, angry, screaming at each other.

Calla has no doubt that the argument actually took place years ago, though she's not sure whether she witnessed it herself or is psychically channeling it.

"*. . . because I promised I'd never tell . . .*" Mom sobs.

"*. . . for your own good . . .*" Odelia says, and then, "*. . . how you can live with yourself . . .*"

Then one of them—Calla isn't sure which—declares, with chilling certainty: *"The only way we'll learn the truth is to dredge the lake."*

Now that she knows what she knows about Mom and Darrin's past . . .

Calla thoughtfully watches Odelia pour coffee, chatting easily with Dad.

Does she know about the baby?

And what does dredging the lake have to do with anything?

Calla no longer smells lilies of the valley, but maybe Aiyana will come to her with some kind of message, like she has in the past.

Abruptly, she pushes back her chair.

Gammy asks, "Where are you going?"

To find Aiyana.

"Can I call Jacy?"

Seeing the dubious expression on both their faces, Calla realizes she probably should have said she was calling Evangeline instead.

But she and Evangeline aren't exactly on friendly terms these days—all the more reason Dad's stay next door will be awkward.

Well, if not Evangeline, then Calla should have said she was calling someone else. Someone who wasn't an accomplice in her mission to Geneseo and her lie to her grandmother.

Now, whenever she's with Jacy, the two of them, Gammy and Dad, are going to think she's sneaking around behind their backs. Great.

It's her father who speaks up first. "Go ahead. Go call Jacy."

"Thanks."

As she leaves the kitchen, she realizes she was really asking her grandmother's permission—not his. She's been answering to Gammy ever since she moved here. Dad, living thousands of miles away, hasn't had much say over what she does on a daily basis.

That, of course, is no longer the case.

Now she'll have to report to both Dad and Gammy—and they'll be total watchdogs after all she's been through. She'll be lucky if they let her go away to college next fall.

Which reminds her . . .

She's supposed to be narrowing down her choices and meeting with her guidance counselor about it in a few days.

Not to mention, she's got a pile of weekend homework to get to before tomorrow morning.

The last thing she feels like doing right now is worrying about any of that.

Jacy . . . I really do need to talk to Jacy.

She swings through the living room to grab the cordless phone receiver, then heads up the stairs with it, her duffel, *and* her mother's laptop. She'll hide that away until she feels like dealing with whatever additional information might be buried in its files.

Gert is waiting at the top of the stairs.

"Hi, kitty. Did you miss me? Hmm?"

The cat rubs against Calla's legs, purring.

"I know. . . . I missed you, too." Calla reaches down to stroke her soft fur. "Do you want to sleep on my bed tonight?"

Abruptly, Gert arches her back and thrusts her paws forward on the floor.

Calla laughs. "Is that a yes?"

Then she realizes Gert has fastened her feline gaze on something over Calla's shoulder. She turns just in time to see a filmy apparition drift into the wall.

They really are everywhere.

This morning the airport—and the plane, too—were loaded with spirits along for the ride, drawn by the passengers' nervous energy, no doubt.

If there's anything Calla has learned lately about the dearly departed, it's that in order to manifest, their spirits feed off human—and sometimes electrical, or technological—energy.

And that animals are particularly aware of their presence.

Gert is still keeping a wary eye on the wall where the

apparition disappeared. There was originally a doorway there, Gammy told Calla.

"It's okay, Gert." She leans over to pet the kitten. "It's just, you know, a . . . visitor. You'll get used to them, like me. Well, I mean, I'm trying to."

Gert looks at the wall, and then at Calla for another long moment, before turning and strolling down the stairs.

Feeling depleted, Calla steps over the threshold into Mom's girlhood bedroom, with its old-fashioned white beadboard and striped wallpaper and sage-and-rose color scheme.

As she sets her belongings on the floor and inhales the familiar smell of old wood and clean linens, an unexpected wave of relief washes over her.

There's Mom's white iron twin bed covered in a patchwork quilt pieced together from Mom's little-girl dresses. There's Mom's carved wooden music box filled with her jewelry. There are Mom's childhood books on the shelves, progressing from the Little House series to *The Outsiders* to *Flowers in the Attic*.

And there, Calla realizes with a jolt, is Mom herself.

Mom, not as Calla knew her, but as she appeared at Calla's age, when she lived here. When she looked so much like Calla does now—same slim, long-waisted build; same wide-set hazel eyes; same thick, milk-chocolate-colored hair streaked with lighter shades of brown—that if they were facing each other, it would be like gazing into a mirror.

She's lying on her stomach on the bed, reading a book—one of the Little House books, Calla sees. Her legs are bent at the knees, feet waving lazily in the air, as though she hasn't a care in the world.

Then, as abruptly as the apparition appeared, she's gone.

"Mom! Mom, wait!" Calla rushes toward the bed, arms outstretched.

But the room is empty. The bed is empty. She's all alone.

Trembling, she sinks onto the mattress and touches the spot where she saw her mother.

Jacy once mentioned a theory that events can leave psychic imprints on the places where they occurred.

That's what must have happened; it's as if a door opened just long enough for Calla to glimpse the past before it was slammed shut again.

Calla didn't *feel* Mom's presence, though.

Not the way she's felt other spirits. Kaitlyn Riggs, for instance—the girl who was kidnapped and murdered. Or her schoolmate Donald Reamer's dead father. Or Aiyana . . .

Those were all visitations.

She's been waiting for one from her mother.

But this was more like . . . looking at an old snapshot.

An odd snapshot, really, because the book in Mom's hands was meant for a much younger reader. Not that it matters.

"Mom, can you hear me? I need to see you. *Really* see you. The way I knew you. I need to feel you here. I need you to come to me, please. I need to know what happened."

I need . . . I need . . . I need . . .

Calla sinks onto the bed and buries her face in her hands, frustrated.

She needs answers.

Why is it that finding out who killed her mother only opened the door to more questions?

Like . . . what happened to her mother's other child?

There are only three options, really. Either Mom and Darrin gave the baby up for adoption, or Darrin raised it himself, or . . .

It died.

She glances at the laptop.

There's a chance she could log in right now and find out that she has a brother or sister living in Boston or something.

Are you ready for that, though?

Calla hesitates.

Not yet.

Not right this minute, anyway.

First things first.

With a trembling hand, she dials Jacy's phone number.

FOUR

Lily Dale
Monday, October 8
3:33 p.m.

"I really can't stick around for very long," Calla informs her grandmother and father as the three of them walk out the door and down the front steps beneath an ominous sky. "I've got to study, and then I'm meeting Jacy for a little while."

When she called him earlier, he was headed out the door with his foster dads and couldn't talk.

"Are they right there with you?" she asked. "Because I can talk, and you can listen. There's some stuff I want to tell you."

"Tell me in person. I'll come over when I get back."

"How about if we just meet down by the lake at five o'clock or so?" she suggested instead.

She isn't exactly eager for Jacy to come face-to-face

with Gammy and Dad now that they know about his part in her lie.

"Make it five fifteen," Jacy told her, and she reluctantly agreed, wondering how she's going to last that long without telling someone the whole shocking story and asking for advice.

"Listen, I know you've got a life here, and you're busy with your friends and schoolwork—hopefully not in that order," Dad says, patting her shoulder as they cross the yard toward the Taggarts' porch. "I just wanted you to come over and see where I'll be staying, that's all."

Calla bites her tongue to keep from saying that she's seen the Taggarts' guest room plenty of times, and even spent the night in it a few weeks ago when she and Evangeline had a sleepover.

Brat, she scolds herself. *What you really want to tell him is that* you *belong here . . .* he *doesn't.*

Yeah, but only because you know he's going to freak and want to leave when he finds out what really goes on in this town.

Which is bound to happen any second now, when Dad notices . . .

Wait a minute.

The shingle that ordinarily hangs beside Ramona's door—the one that reads RAMONA TAGGART, REGISTERED MEDIUM—seems to be missing.

Calla raises an eyebrow at her grandmother and gestures with her head at the empty bracket overhead.

"I asked her to take it down for a few days." Gammy's whisper is muffled by a rumble of thunder in the west. "Just until your father gets settled in."

Calla—who was grateful when her grandmother did the same thing with ODELIA LAUDER, REGISTERED MEDIUM whenever Dad came to visit—now wonders uneasily whether it's a good idea to deliberately keep him in the dark.

If he's going to freak out and leave, it's better to just get it over with, isn't it?

Maybe we should all just come out and tell him. About Gammy, and Ramona, and . . . me.

"Hello, hello! Come on in before it rains!" Ramona calls out, and Calla looks up to see that she's waiting in the open doorway, beckoning them.

Well, she *is* psychic. She was probably aware they were on their way the very second they finished washing the lunch dishes and headed for the door.

Or maybe she's been eagerly watching for them since Gammy called her a good half hour ago to say that Dad had accepted her invitation to stay here.

That's more what it seems like, really.

Ramona, wearing one of her gypsy-style dresses, is all but bouncing with excitement as she holds the door open for them, chattering a mile a minute.

"Welcome back, Calla! And I'm so glad to see you again, Jeff. What happened in Florida? Odelia said something about a problem down there, but—you'll have to fill me in. Come in, ignore the mess, come right up the stairs," she says, leading the way up the narrow flight with the three of them trooping behind her. "Watch your head at the landing, there, Jeff. Like I told Odelia, it's not the Ritz, but it's a place to sleep and, hey, it's free."

"No, please, you have to let me pay you. If I were staying at a hotel, I'd be paying."

"True, but at a hotel, you'd have maid service. Have you looked around? There's no maid here," Ramona says wryly. "No ice machine, no room service, no pool . . ."

"Darn," Dad says. "How about nightly turndown service with a towel swan and chocolate on the pillow?"

"Hmm . . . maybe that could be arranged."

They're flirting. It's so weird. Calla turns to glance at her grandmother to see if she's noticed. Yup. There's a thoughtful expression on Odelia's face and a gleam in her eye.

They pass the open doorway to Evangeline's room, then her brother's. "Company, Mason," Ramona calls to her nephew, who's sprawled on his bed with a handheld computer game.

Looking at Mason is like looking at Evangeline—rather, looking at her if she wore owlish glasses, had frizzy, close-cropped red hair, and was perpetually fixated on a book or a screen of some sort.

"Say hello, Mason."

"Hello." His hazel eyes never leave the game.

"Remember Calla's dad, Jeff? He's going to be staying in the guest room for a while."

"Uh-huh."

Ramona sighs. "He's normally much more communicative."

He is? Calla's never witnessed it, but who knows? Maybe Mason turns into a real live wire when she's not around.

"I'll see you later, huh, Mason?" Dad says.

Mason—who lost both his parents before he was old

37

enough to remember them—actually looks up. "Sure. See you later."

Watching the two exchange a brief smile before Ramona leads the group down the hall again, Calla can't help but feel a tiny flicker of jealousy.

It suddenly occurs to her that Mason—and Evangeline, too—will be sharing a house with her father now. And that she herself won't be.

She had thought it would be a good thing to keep him at arm's length, but maybe she was wrong. Maybe she's missed him too much for that.

"This is it," Ramona announces, and opens the door to the guest room with a jangle of bracelets.

There's a bed, dresser, and small bedside table that holds a fan of magazines and a vase of purple asters obviously cut from the clump growing beside the Taggarts' front porch.

"This is charming," Dad declares, and turns to Calla. "What do you think?"

"Charming," she agrees.

"And the best part of all is that your dad will be right next door," Ramona drapes an arm around Calla's shoulders and squeezes her. "I know how much you two have missed each other."

"We have. Thanks, Ra—" Calla breaks off, stunned to see one of the magazines flying off the bedside table. It seems to hover in midair before landing on the floor at her feet.

Her father, with his back to the table, didn't see what happened, but Odelia and Ramona did. They exchange a nervous glance.

"I must have bumped into this. I'm such a klutz. Oh

well, my secret is out," Ramona says lightly, reaching for the magazine.

Her secret is out?

Calla braces herself, thinking she's about to reveal her supernatural abilities.

Her grandmother obviously thinks the same thing because she shoots Ramona a look of dismay.

"What secret is that?" Dad asks with interest.

"That I'm the ultimate pack rat. I never throw anything away. See?"

Calla all but sighs in relief as Ramona holds up the magazine's cover. On it is a photograph of a smiling, familiar woman and the headline AN INTERVIEW WITH NEW FIRST LADY LAURA BUSH.

"Well, there's nothing wrong with outdated reading material," comments Odelia, whose cluttered coffee table brings to mind a dentist's waiting room. "Right, Calla?"

"Right," she murmurs, and looks around the room for a wanton spirit who might be responsible for the mishap.

She can't see anything, but that doesn't mean there's no one around.

"I'm a pack rat, too," Dad comments. "It used to drive my wife crazy."

There's a moment of awkward silence.

"It didn't bother Mom all that much, Dad," Calla feels obligated to say. "As long as you kept your mess out of her way."

"Stephanie liked things to be organized," Gammy explains to Ramona.

"I wish I could be like that. Me, I'm just the opposite."

"Same here."

Ramona and Dad smile at each other.

Calla and her grandmother look at each other.

She's thinking what I'm thinking. She knows something's going to happen between them, too.

Somewhere downstairs, a door slams.

"I'm home, Aunt Ramona!" Evangeline's voice calls. "And Russell's with me, so if you're coming downstairs, make sure you're decent!"

Odelia snorts. "You have a habit of being indecent?"

"Yeah, well, sometimes I'm about to get into the shower and realize I left the oven on or I forgot something, and I run downstairs in a towel," Ramona admits with her usual free-and-easy candor. "But I'll make sure I change that habit now that Jeff is here."

"Oh, don't change your habits on my account," Dad says with a wave of his hand. Then he turns a bright, burning red. "I mean . . . it's not that I want you to be indecent or anything . . . just . . . you know . . . I, uh, I don't want you to, uh . . ."

Under different circumstances, Calla might find it sweet, the way he's stammering and fumbling like a kid with a crush. But he's her father, for Pete's sake, and Ramona is . . . well, *not* her mother. Plus, she's a kooky medium.

Not that *all* mediums are kooky.

But Ramona sure is. She's a total free spirit.

A total free spirit who's definitely looking for love. Ramona has shared plenty of amusing hard-luck dating stories with Calla since they met a few months ago.

Which is part of the reason Calla has always liked her so much . . . until right about now.

"Aunt Ramona?" Evangeline calls again from downstairs. "Anybody home?"

"I'll be right down! And I'm not alone so I hope you're decent!" Grinning, Ramona leads the way back to the first floor.

Calla really wishes she hadn't allowed Dad and Gammy to drag her over here. Evangeline hasn't exactly forgiven her for going out with Jacy, her longtime crush. Still, when they saw each other at school on Thursday, Calla did her best to make amends, and Evangeline seemed to melt just a little.

There she is, waiting at the foot of the stairs with Russell Lancione, the "blah" (according to Evangeline) guy who's hopelessly infatuated with her. Evangeline said she doesn't want him to like her that way, but Calla's not so sure. They look pretty happy, laughing together.

Evangeline's round freckled face and hazel eyes seem to be accented with makeup, and her kinky reddish orange hair is becomingly pulled back.

"Calla! I didn't know you were here."

"Yup . . . here I am! Hi, guys!" she says brightly with a sweeping windshield-wiper wave. "You, uh, remember my dad, right, Evangeline?"

Duh. It's not like she hasn't met him a bunch of times.

"Hi, Mr. Delaney. I mean, Professor Delaney."

" 'Jeff' is just fine," Dad says with a smile.

Evangeline flashes her usual cheerful smile back, and Calla feels a pang, remembering just how many times her friend has been there for her since she arrived in Lily Dale.

"This is my friend, Russell, Mr.—Jeff."

As Dad and Russell shake hands, Calla longs to just grab on to Evangeline and tell her how much she's missed her. But she's afraid to.

What if Evangeline pushes her away?

Would you really blame her, after what you did?

No. Don't do that to yourself.

You didn't do anything wrong.

It's not as if Jacy had feelings for Evangeline, too, and Calla stole him away. Evangeline would be the first to admit that he was just a friend, no matter how much she wished there could be more between them.

"Jeff's going to be staying here in the guest room for a while, so I was just showing him around," Ramona informs her niece.

"Cool. Hey, Calla, how was Florida?"

Calla looks up in surprise at Evangeline's question. "It was . . ." She glances around at the others. "I'll tell you later."

"Sounds like a long story," Ramona says.

"Definitely." Calla finds herself wishing that Russell weren't here so that she could whisk Evangeline away from the adults and spill the whole sorry mess.

But judging by the way Russell is hovering at her friend's side, he's not going anywhere soon.

Thunder rumbles again outside, and Ramona claps her hands together. "Who wants to go sit on the porch and watch the storm come in over the lake?"

"Um, Russell and I have to go look up some stuff on the computer."

In the old days—like, before Calla admitted she'd kissed Jacy—Evangeline would have asked Calla to join them.

Now, she only drags Russell to the next room with a "See you guys later."

"I hate to ruin the party, but I have an appointment in about twenty minutes," Gammy says, reaching into the breast pocket of her blouse and checking a pocket watch on a gold chain.

Why, Calla wonders—not for the first time—doesn't she wear a Timex on her wrist like the rest of the world? It's not that Calla doesn't appreciate her grandmother for who she is, eccentricities and all, but some of her habits are pretty . . .

Kooky.

Another kooky medium. Go figure.

"Calla? What do you say?" Ramona asks. "Do you have an appointment, too, or do you want to come hang out on the porch?"

"Actually . . ." She glances at her father, sees the way he's looking at Ramona, and promptly feels like a third wheel. "I've got to go study. If you guys don't mind."

No one minds.

Imagine that.

Crossing the yard again with her grandmother as Dad and Ramona settle into wicker rockers, Calla can't help but feel wistful.

More change.

Constant change.

Maybe that's what life is about, but change in small doses is a lot easier to swallow.

"It was pretty interesting," Odelia says, "what happened upstairs with that magazine, don't you think?"

"Oh . . . you mean Ramona knocking it off the table?"

"Ramona didn't knock it off the table."

"She didn't?"

"Are you playing dumb with me, Calla, my dear?"

"Yes," she admits. "I saw it. What do you think it meant?"

Odelia shrugs. "Spirit playing around, most likely. Or maybe trying to tell one of us something."

"What? That it's time for Ramona to update her magazine collection?"

Her grandmother grins. "Could be." She pauses to deadhead a couple of fall blooms along the front path to her door.

Then she straightens and asks, "So, Evangeline has a boyfriend, huh?"

"Not really. He's just her friend."

"That's what you think."

"That's what she thinks, too."

"I don't know about that."

Calla glances sharply at Odelia. "You think she likes him?"

"I know she does." Her grandmother gives a firm nod as they climb the steps. "That's not all I know."

"What do you mean?"

"Nothing. Just . . . Evangeline isn't the only one around here who likes someone."

"You mean me and Jacy? Gammy, I don't want you to—"

"That's not what I meant. But, about last weekend, now that you bring it up . . ."

"Forget I did."

"I don't think so. We have a lot to talk about."

"I know. But not now. You have an appointment."

And I don't feel like defending myself right now.

"We're going to talk," Gammy says, "because you lied to me, and I can't—"

"I know, Gammy, and I'm sorry. I'll explain everything. I promise. I just needed to know. About my mother, and . . ."

Darrin.

Gammy didn't like him.

Ramona told Calla that.

Why not?

It was something about Darrin having negative energy, but maybe there was more to it. Maybe . . .

Surely she doesn't know about the baby . . . does she?

Go ahead. Ask her.

But if Calla asks her . . . and she *doesn't* already know . . .

You'll be opening a whole new can of worms. Is that really what you want to do right now?

Thunder claps so near that it makes Calla jump.

Odelia glances up at the sky. "Come on. Let's get inside. This is going to be nasty."

I'm not ready, Calla decides, following her into the house. *I'm not ready to tell her yet. Not until I know more.*

FIVE

Lily Dale
Monday, October 8
5:13 p.m.

Calla steps around puddles that fill the potholes on Cottage Row, making her way down to the lakefront park beneath a canopy of fall foliage. Leaves and eaves drip pleasantly around her. The storm ended a little while ago, ushering in a tide of warmer, humid air, and she left her fleece jacket at home.

A week or so ago, she was expecting to see her first snow. But striding along in short sleeves with a gentle breeze off the water, as opposed to the usual stiff wind, she realizes that it almost feels like late summer again. Dad might even be able to last another day or two without having to buy a cold-weather wardrobe.

He had returned from Ramona's porch just as she was walking out the door a few minutes ago.

"Hey, Cal', where are you going?" he asked, bounding up the steps like a much younger man.

"I have to meet my friend. I won't be long."

"Jacy?"

"Right."

He nodded. "Ramona said he's a good kid."

She did? Calla raises an eyebrow. "Yeah. He is."

"She said he's had a rough life."

"Yeah. He has." She shifted her weight uncomfortably, wondering why he was discussing her with Ramona—and what else Ramona said about Jacy.

"Be careful out there," was all he said, then went on into Odelia's house to gather his things to move next door.

She probably shouldn't let it bother her—that Ramona was talking about Jacy. Especially since Ramona's stamp of approval has obviously won over her father.

No, she shouldn't *mind*.

It's just that . . .

Well, she's used to being her father's only connection to Lily Dale. She's the one who has—so far—been able to filter what he does and doesn't know.

About Jacy or anything else.

This was just another reminder that Dad is once again part of her day-to-day business. It won't be long before he knows everything about her life here. What then?

You'll have to worry about that when it comes up, she tells herself. *You've got enough on your plate right now.*

The lake water has become a choppy blue-black in the wake of the storm. Calla can see Jacy waiting for her, leaning against the wooden railing in the pavilion where they usually meet.

A baseball cap rides backward over his short black hair. His running shorts reveal muscular legs and a weathered gray T-shirt exposes tanned biceps.

Wow. He looks good.

Um, no. He looks *great*.

Calla's heart picks up its pace, and so do her feet.

Just before she reaches him, though, she stops short, suddenly feeling shy.

"Hi."

"Hi."

They look at each other for a long moment. Then Jacy shocks her by grabbing her in a fierce embrace.

"Thank God you're okay," he says into her hair. "Thank God."

Surprised, she asks, "Are you okay?"

"Yeah. I just didn't realize that I . . . until . . . I mean . . . I guess . . ."

Say it, Jacy, she begs silently. *Say what you're thinking. Tell me what you're feeling.*

He doesn't.

That's not his style.

She knows he's learned the hard way not to reveal his emotions. Having grown up on the reservation with abusive parents, Jacy Bly doesn't trust many people—if anyone at all. Maybe not even Peter and Walt, his foster dads.

Maybe not even me, she acknowledges as he pulls back,

lets her go. But when she looks up at him, what she sees in his dark eyes startles her almost as much as the emotional greeting.

He cares about her.

A lot.

Not just as a fellow medium, or even just as a friend concerned for her well-being.

He cares the way she's dreamed of him caring.

He doesn't have to say it. She can see it and feel it. Words are unimportant.

"The thing that gets me is that I knew it." Jacy shakes his head. "I *knew* it was going to be the water."

"I know you did."

He tried to warn her before she left—that he'd been having visions of her struggling in water. Dylan, her five-year-old babysitting charge, had a similar premonition.

But what was she supposed to do with that information?

She's been thinking about that for the last few days.

About the warnings from Jacy, and from Dylan, and for all she knows from Odelia, who might also have seen something foretelling Calla's near-drowning, considering her cryptic demands that Calla stay out of Cassadaga Lake.

As if she could have kept a promise to never go swimming there—ever. Or as if she could have . . . whatever. Moved to the desert? Gone around wearing a life jacket on dry land for the rest of her life, just in case?

What could she do?

That's the problem with this premonition stuff.

You might know what's going to happen . . . but it's going to happen. That's the whole point. You can't change it, no matter what—at least, not that Calla has seen. You can't stop it from happening.

You can only dread it.

And wonder when it's going to happen.

"I swear," Jacy says, "if this had ended any other way . . ."

"But it didn't. It all worked out."

"Yeah, I know, but Calla . . ." He puts an arm around her shoulder, his feet straddling hers as he leans against the railing, pulling her back against his chest. "What would I do without you?"

She looks up at him.

"I don't want to be without you, okay? Not anymore."

"Well, I'm not going back to Florida for a while, so . . ."

"That's not what I mean." He puts a gentle hand beneath her chin and tilts her face up toward his.

His kiss is soft and sweet and oh, so fleeting. It's over before she can absorb what's happened, and it's all she can do to keep from touching her hands to her lips, dazed.

He nods, as if they've just settled something.

Maybe, she realizes, they just have.

He strokes her hair, and she rests her head against his shoulder. Until this moment, she didn't know how much she's longed for a physical connection to someone, didn't remember how good it feels to have someone to lean on, literally.

"You said you had stuff to tell me," Jacy says after a few minutes.

"Yeah." She tries to remember what it was. Not easy, with him so close she can feel his breath stirring her hair.

Reluctantly, she pulls back so that she can think straight.

"I really need your advice, and there's no one else I can tell."

"Is it about what happened with that woman?"

"Sort of."

When she called him from Florida Saturday, she'd filled him in about what Sharon Logan did to her. And, presumably, to her mother.

But Jacy doesn't know about the e-mails.

Or about the baby.

She tells him now, eventually going from leaning against Jacy to facing him, laying it all out in a detached, matter-of-fact tone.

As if she's talking about total strangers, and not her very own mother.

And her very own sister or brother.

He's quiet for a long time.

"Say something," she begs at last.

He reaches out and grabs her hand, squeezing it. "I don't know what to say. Are you okay with all this?"

"Not really. Would you be?"

He answers her question with another question. "What happened to the baby?"

"I don't know. I haven't read the rest of the e-mail yet."

"Are you serious?" At her nod, he asks, "But why not?"

"For one thing, because I don't want my father to know about it, and he's been watching me like a prison guard twenty-four-seven."

"He's not here now."

"Neither is the laptop."

"You can check it when you go back to Odelia's, though. Unless you don't want to."

"I do, it's just . . . I guess I'm afraid of what I'm going to find out. And I'm definitely dreading what will happen when my father finds out."

"Don't tell him."

"But I have to. I mean, I can't go the rest of my life keeping this deep dark secret from him."

"Your mother did."

She blinks. "That's different."

"Not really." Jacy lets go of her hand and raises his to hold off her protest. "Let's say you tell your father. . . . And then what?"

"What do you mean?"

"What will happen? If he finds out, I mean?"

"You know. . . . He'll be upset."

"How much more upset can he be than he already is? Hasn't the worst already happened? She's dead."

"Yeah, but . . . she was in love with another man."

"You don't know that for sure."

"She had a child with him."

"Years ago. It was over. She was married to your father."

"I know, but . . . I mean, you didn't read the e-mail. She said it was incredible to see Darrin again. She was lying to me and my father about where she was, saying she was away on a business trip when she was sneaking off to meet him. Do you really think they were just friends?"

He doesn't answer that.

She does. "I know they weren't. They were still in love."

"Yeah, well . . . nobody's perfect."

"Nobody's perfect?" Calla's eyebrows shoot up. "What kind of thing is that to say?"

"It's true."

She hates his reasonable tone of voice, hates that he isn't outraged with her. How can he sit here discussing it like they're talking about her mother switching brands of laundry soap?

"You can't possibly think it was *okay*, what my mother did?"

"There are a lot of worse things," he says flatly, "a mother can do. Much worse."

Oh.

Right.

"I'm sorry," she tells Jacy, whose mother, she heard, neglected and abused him. Calla doesn't know the details, and she hasn't felt comfortable asking. She lost custody. Signed adoption papers to give him away to someone else.

"Why are you sorry?"

"Because . . ." She shrugs. She can't say it. He doesn't need to hear it.

Here comes that defensive expression of his again, rolling in like storm clouds. She's seen it before.

She touches his arm.

Ordinarily, he might have shaken her off, or at least, have failed to respond.

But they've turned a corner. He looks up at her and nods, as though he knows exactly what she's thinking.

"You can't change what happened to me, Calla. You can make a lot of things better for me. But not the past."

"I know. And the same goes for me. You can't really blame me for wanting to protect my dad from what she did."

"I don't blame you. Maybe you're protecting yourself, too."

"What do you mean?"

He shrugs. "I mean . . . maybe *you're* the one who doesn't want to know the truth."

"Me? I want to know. *Of course* I want to know."

"Okay."

"I went all the way to Florida," she informs him, "and I almost got myself *killed*, because I want to know."

"Okay."

"You don't think I'm the least bit curious about the fact that I might have a sister or brother?"

"You didn't read the rest of her e-mail."

"Not yet. But I was going to. I was going to . . . tonight."

Except that she wasn't.

Not tonight.

Maybe not even tomorrow.

It's still so raw.

"You don't have to find out the rest of the story, you know," Jacy says quietly. "It is what it is. You can just leave the e-mail alone and remember your mother the way she was."

"Except that I have a half sibling somewhere in this world."

"Are you sure about that?"

"They had a baby together."

"Did Darrin raise it?"

"It's possible. But Darrin's dead. I don't know how I can find out now."

"You could ask his parents about it."

"His parents? You think they know? Do you think my grandmother knows, too?"

"You won't find out unless you ask."

"I know, but if I ask—and they didn't know—then . . . they'll know."

He's silent.

"I guess I could ask," she says slowly.

"You said you wanted to go talk to the Yateses this week, before they leave for the winter, and tell them Darrin's dead. I'll go with you. We'll do it together."

"Is that really up to us, though?" She thought it was, back when she found the article on the Internet that stated Darrin had died last June in an unsolved murder. Now she wasn't so sure.

Jacy gives her a level look. "We're probably the only two people alive who know that Tom Leolyn was really Darrin Yates. Are we really going to let those old people wonder for the rest of their lives whatever happened to their son?"

"No! I wouldn't do that." She hesitates. "I'm just afraid to face them. Remember when they told us that they sense he's still on the earth plane? How are they going to react when they find out they're wrong?"

"It won't be easy for anyone, but I'll go with you, like I said the other day. We'll show them the death notice from the newspaper, and we'll tell them what you found out."

"What, we're going to just march over there and break the news that their son is dead? What do we do when they start screaming in grief? Because that's what people do when someone they love dies, you know."

That's what I did.

She doesn't say that part, though; just presses her fingertips to her temples, telling Jacy, "I have a pounding headache, and I can't even think straight."

He wraps his arms around her again. "That's no surprise. You've been through a lot."

She swallows hard. There's a lump in her throat.

Everything feels wrong in her life—everything but Jacy. Nothing is familiar—not this relationship. Not even herself. What happened to sweet, nice, easygoing Calla?

She's turned into a stranger. And so has her mother.

"You said you wanted my advice, right?"

"Right," she tells Jacy in a small voice.

"Here it is: go home and eat dinner and get some sleep tonight and forget all this for right now." He tilts to press his forehead against hers. "It's too much for you to handle. You can figure it all out later, and I'll be there to help you."

"That," Calla says gratefully, "might be the best advice I've ever heard."

"Calla?"

Startled, she opens her eyes to find herself fully clothed on her bed in her lamplit room, an open textbook lying near her cheek. Rain is falling hard on the roof, pinging into the gutter outside her window.

Her grandmother is in the doorway, telephone in hand. "It's not even nine o'clock yet. Are you sleeping already?"

"No, I . . . I mean, I guess I dozed off while I was studying."

"It's Lisa." Odelia waves the receiver. "Do you want me to tell her to call you back tomorrow?"

Yes. She really does. She's too drowsy to chat right now.

But Lisa can probably hear every word they're saying. She'll be hurt if Calla doesn't take the call.

Reluctantly, she sits up. "It's okay, I'll talk to her."

As she holds out her hand, the lights flicker a little.

Calla glances around, half expecting to see an apparition. Sometimes their energy interferes with the electricity.

The room is empty, and distant thunder tells her the weather is responsible this time.

Gammy looks at the window. "It's really pouring out there. It's not a good idea to talk on the phone during a storm. Make it quick, okay?"

"Okay." Hiding a yawn, she takes the receiver.

"And get some sleep after you hang up," Gammy tells her, planting a kiss on her forehead. "You need to rest."

"I will." She waits until her grandmother has left the room, closing the door behind her. "Lisa? Hi."

"Hi," Lisa drawls back. It comes out *Ha–ah*. "How were your flights this morning? Everything on time?"

"Pretty much. We had a great view of Manhattan when we landed there. The pilot described everything. I was sitting on the left side of the plane, like you said I should, so I got to see all the good stuff."

"Did you see the Empire State Building?"

"And the Statue of Liberty and Rockefeller Center . . ."

"Cool."

"Yeah." She hesitates. "It was really good to spend time with you, Lis'—I mean, other than what happened."

"You, too. I'm sorry I got so upset with you when you didn't want to come to the senior class car wash with me Saturday morning."

"It's okay."

"I just didn't get why you'd want to go poking around

your old house after everything you went through there. I had no idea something like that was going to happen to you or I would have gone with you in a heartbeat. You know that, right?"

"I know, Lis'. It's really okay." Calla paces across the rose-and-sage-colored braided rug, phone in hand, feeling groggy.

"I feel so bad."

Calla can't help but smile. Lisa really is a good friend. A good, and now guilt-ridden, friend.

"Listen," she says, "if it makes you feel any better, if I had any idea what I was walking into there, I would have definitely gone to the senior car wash instead."

Lisa laughs. "If you had, you would have seen Brittany Jensen in Daisy Dukes and the skimpiest bikini top ever, trying to win back Nick Rodriguez. But guess what? He called this afternoon and asked me out."

"That's great! You've been hoping for that."

As Lisa recaps the conversation she had with Nick word for word, Calla leans her forehead against the window glass, looking out into the night. She can't see much because of the glare—just tree branches swaying in the wet gusts.

"Oh, and Calla, you so have to check out Nick's MySpace page when you get a chance. There's this great picture of him surfing."

"I wish I could see it."

"I thought you were online again. You said you were bringing your mom's laptop back with you!"

"Oh . . . right."

Funny. There was actually a time when she wanted the laptop just so that she could stay plugged in to her old life.

"Check out Nick's page. And then IM me and tell me what you think of the picture."

"Okay, I—"

A flash of lightning illuminates the landscape.

For a fleeting moment, she can clearly see a male figure standing in the yard below, looking up at her.

Darrin Yates.

Heart pounding, Calla gasps and jumps back from the window.

"Calla? Are you okay?"

"Yeah, it was just . . . lightning. We're having a storm." She pulls the shade, knowing it won't really keep him out if he wants to get to her. He's been in this room before.

Back when she didn't realize he was visiting from the other side.

"Lisa, I should get off the phone."

"Okay. Make sure you check out Nick's page, though."

"I will," she says absently, and lifts the edge of the shade to peer into the night, looking for Darrin.

Rather, Darrin's spirit.

"Oh, and my brother said he e-mailed you, too."

"He did?" That captures her attention.

"Make sure you e-mail him back, okay? He's really worried about you."

Calla doesn't know what to say to that. Or how to feel about it.

Too little, too late is how she would have reacted just days ago about Kevin, her ex-boyfriend, trying to reach out to her again after breaking up with her and dating someone new.

But after staying under the same roof with him while she

was in Florida—and after having a heart-to-heart talk with him Friday night, before everything happened—she isn't so sure.

He broke up with Annie, his new girlfriend.

And the last thing he said to Calla that night was, *"Don't write me off just yet. Promise me you won't."*

She didn't make any promises.

But she didn't tell him to forget it, either.

Why not? Is it wrong to feel a connection—however slight—to Kevin when her feelings for Jacy are so strong?

Caring about someone new doesn't mean you automatically stop caring about someone else you once loved, advises a voice in Calla's head—a voice that isn't her own.

She can hear her mother saying the words so clearly that she wonders, for a moment, if it's something Mom actually told her back when she was still alive.

If it is, though, she can't remember when, or why, her mother would have said it.

Thunder booms and, again, Calla peeks through the window—just in time to see lightning spark temporary daylight again.

The spot where Darrin was standing is empty now.

But he isn't far away.

Calla can feel his presence crackling in the air, as palpable as the electric storm outside.

"Lisa, I really have to go," she says, keeping an eye out for him as she moves across the room, away from the window.

"Okay. Be safe. Love you."

"You, too."

She hangs up the phone and tosses it onto the bed.

Then, after hesitating for a moment, she bends over and looks underneath it.

No Darrin.

Feeling a little sheepish, she straightens and goes over to the case that holds her mother's laptop. As she picks it up, she wonders if this is a good idea.

She really is exhausted.

Maybe she should just forget it tonight, crawl into bed, turn out the light, and go to sleep. . . .

With the spirit of her mother's dead lover hanging around as if he's trying to tell her something.

Yawning deeply, she weighs the laptop in her hand, along with the decision.

Should she follow Jacy's advice and wait, at least until tomorrow, when she's better equipped to deal with it?

Or should she find out the truth right now?

Now, she decides. The sooner she finds out the rest of the story, the sooner Darrin—and perhaps Aiyana—will leave her alone, and she'll get closure and move on.

Or the sooner she'll be able to find her sister or brother.

Mind made up, Calla opens the laptop, presses the power switch, and waits for it to boot up.

Nervously, she looks around the room. Still no sign of Darrin.

But that doesn't mean he isn't here, watching.

It takes her a moment to realize nothing's happening with the computer.

Then she remembers: when she packed it away in Florida,

she was in a hurry. She probably didn't bother to turn it off. She must have drained the battery.

Please, please, please, let that be the problem.

It would be easy to fix.

What if it's something more serious? she wonders as she pulls the power cord out of the laptop case.

What if the hard drive or the motherboard or whatever you call it crashed, and all the files have been lost?

Then she'll never know the truth.

Please, please, please . . .

Calla inserts the power cord into the laptop, then drops to her hands and knees with the plug, looking for an outlet.

There's one—and, how convenient, there's the phone jack, right next to it.

All she has to do is—

A deafening crash of thunder . . . and the room is plunged into blackness.

Almost immediately a siren kicks in somewhere outside, an eerie wail in the night.

Whoa.

She hears her grandmother calling her from downstairs. "Calla?"

"Up here, Gammy."

"That must have struck a transformer. Looks like the whole town is dark. Don't move. I'm coming up to find the—*oof.*"

Hearing a thud, Calla cries out, "Gammy?"

"I'm okay. I just walked into something."

"Be careful! Do you want me to come down?"

"No, I'm coming up. Just stay where you—*oof.*"

"Gammy!"

"I'm okay, I'm okay." Odelia mutters a curse under her breath and the steps creak as she painstakingly ascends.

A few minutes—and *oofs* and curses—later, she appears in the doorway, accompanied by a blinding beam.

"What is that, a searchlight?" Calla shields her eyes with her forearm.

"It's a miner's hat. I used to live in coal mine country, remember?"

"West Virginia?"

"Pennsylvania."

"I didn't know that. Don't you have a regular flashlight?"

"This is better. It leaves the hands free."

Yeah, for coal mining.

"I have one for you, too," Odelia says, and the blinding light comes closer. "Put it on and we'll go downstairs and eat all the ice cream in the freezer."

"What? Why?"

"So that it won't melt and go to waste. Here you go."

Calla obediently puts on the miner's hat her grandmother hands her, asking, "How long do you think it'll be before the power comes back on?"

"Oh, you never know. Sometimes just a few minutes. Once in a while, though, we're out for a few days."

"A few days?!"

"Hopefully it won't be that long."

Hopefully not.

But you're probably not going to get into the laptop tonight, Calla tells herself, following her grandmother down to the kitchen.

As she scoops Ben & Jerry's Coffee Heath Bar Crunch into a bowl in the beam of her miner's flashlight, she can't help but wonder if she isn't just a little bit grateful, deep down inside, to put off delving into her mother's secrets once more.

SIX

The dream begins the same as it always has.

She's walking along a grassy shore beside lapping blue water. It's not a big lake; she can see the opposite shore not far in the distance, rimmed by rolling hills. The sky is blue and the sun is shining.

There are lots of tall trees to cast dappled shade around her as she walks.

Nearby, she can see clusters of cottages. Victorian-style, with shutters and fish-scale shingles; cupolas or mansard roofs; porches with gingerbread trim.

There are flowers everywhere. The air is heavy with their

perfume; they bloom in crowded garden beds, spill from window boxes and hanging pots.

They're even here, beneath her feet, growing in a clump on the grassy shore.

These flowers have short, slender, sturdy stems fringed with tiny bell-shaped white blossoms.

Lilies of the valley.

She found a photo in a horticulture book months ago, when the dream first began to haunt her.

As she bends to pick one of the fragile blooms, the sun slips behind a cloud. Thunder rumbles in the distance as she raises the flower to inhale its fragrance, and all at once, she can hear voices. Female voices.

She can't see them, and she can't hear most of what they're saying, but what she does hear is disturbing:

". . . because I promised I'd never tell . . ."

". . . for your own good . . . don't know how you can live with yourself . . ."

"The only way we'll learn the truth is to dredge the lake."

She gazes out over the lake to see that the water has turned black, churning ominously beneath a stormy sky.

Now the women are crying, eerie wails that echo until the storm blows in to drown them out.

Who are they?

Where are they?

Why are they arguing? Why are they crying?

And why, Laura wonders, every time she wakes from the dream, chilled to the bone, do I keep having the same strange dream, over and over?

SEVEN

Lily Dale
Tuesday, October 9
7:50 a.m.

"Morning, Calla!"

Startled to hear a voice as she slips out her grandmother's front door with her backpack, Calla spins around to see her father over on Ramona's porch.

"Dad!"

"That was some storm last night, huh?"

She nods. "When did the power come back on?"

"Around midnight."

"Oh." By that time, she had eaten herself into Coffee Heath Bar Crunch–induced oblivion, too zonked out to even dream.

Seeing movement out of the corner of her eye, she turns and spots a translucent little boy perched in a tree beside Ramona's porch. He's wearing a 1930s-style newsboy hat and knickers, and she's pretty sure she's seen him hanging around before.

"Are you wearing that to school?"

She looks down at her jeans, long sleeved T-shirt, and sneakers. "Um . . . yes?"

"Really."

"It's a public school, Dad," she reminds him. As opposed to a private school: at Shoreside Day back in Florida, she had to wear a preppy uniform every day.

"So everyone dresses down for school? Is that it?"

"Pretty much. Why?"

The little boy in the tree crosses his eyes at her and giggles.

"I just want to make sure that with your mother gone you're not . . . you know . . ."

"Letting my fashion sense go down the tubes?" she asks her father dryly. "That would be tragic."

He snorts.

"What are you doing out here, anyway, Dad?"

"Guess."

She descends a few steps and peers closer at him across her grandmother's unkempt hedges, still glistening from last night's rain.

Dad is sitting on a wicker rocker, clasping a coffee mug in both hands. His hair stands straight up, he's got a face full of razor stubble, and he's wearing a pair of sweatpants and a rumpled T-shirt, looking like he just rolled out of bed five minutes ago.

"I have no idea what you're doing. Why don't you tell me?"

"Nothing." He grins. "I'm doing absolutely *nothing* but relaxing. Enjoying the beautiful morning." He waves a hand at the sun slanting down through the misty treetops, a rare sight around here. "And I get to see my daughter off to school. What do you think about that?"

"It's . . . uh, great."

"You know, Cal', I don't know what I was thinking. Why have I just spent the last few months alone, on the opposite end of the country from the one person I care about? It doesn't make sense."

Ramona. Is he talking about Ramona?

Is that what he's trying to tell me?

Are he and Ramona in love?

Has he been having a secret affair with her since they met?

"I don't know why I didn't figure out until now that the two of us belong together, after all we've been through lately."

Dad has been tragically widowed, but Ramona . . . her latest boyfriend dumped her for a Buffalo Jill. How does that compare? Clearly, he's lost touch with reality.

"Dad, are you okay?"

"I will be now that I can start every day by saying good morning to my girl in person. . . ."

His *girl?*

Jealousy streaks through Calla.

Ramona is his girl now?

That's what he always used to call . . .

Oh.

You idiot.

"That's great, Dad," she says with a relieved grin. "I'm glad you're here, too."

How could she even think he was talking about Ramona, when they barely know each other?

I'm his girl. I'm the one he belongs with after all we've been through.

Of course that's what he meant.

Duh.

How could she have thought otherwise? Just because Dad and Ramona are staying under the same roof now . . .

The screen door squeaks next door and Calla looks up just in time to see Ramona step out onto the porch. Her long, curly brown hair is tousled and she's carrying a coffee mug. And wearing a snug-fitting pair of pink pajamas that look awesome on her.

"Morning, Calla!" she calls, waving. Then she turns and says something to Dad that Calla can't hear, and he laughs.

Hmm. They do look pretty cozy over there.

And Calla can try all she wants to ignore it, but her sixth sense is telling her that Folgers isn't all that's brewing next door.

"I've got to get to school," she announces, and heads down the walk toward the street.

The little boy is now dangling from his knees on a branch high above her head, gleefully swinging back and forth.

You're going to get hurt doing that, she tells him silently.

He sticks out his tongue.

Whatever. How hurt can he get? He's already dead.

"Hey, Calla, wait for Evangeline. She's right here!" calls her father, who obviously hasn't heard the news bulletin about the two of them not walking to school together in over a week.

Before Calla can fill him in, Evangeline pops out the door, dressed almost identically to Calla and carrying a backpack.

"Calla! Hi!"

She looks almost pleasantly surprised, so Calla dares to say, "Hi—want to walk to school?"

"Sure."

"Great!"

As Evangeline joins her, Calla can't help but note that it doesn't necessarily mean she's oozing with forgiveness. After all, they're both going in the same direction at the same time. What was Evangeline supposed to say? *No, I want to walk a few steps behind you?*

Which, incidentally, is pretty much what she did all last week.

They head in silence down the road toward the gates. The moment they're out of earshot, Calla says, kicking a pebble along with the toe of her sneaker, "If you don't want to walk with me, it's okay."

"It is? You mean you won't, like, collapse in a heap on the ground and cry?"

Startled, she looks up—and is relieved to see Evangeline's familiar, crinkly grin. "I don't know, I might collapse, but I've cried so many tears over you I think I've run dry."

Evangeline laughs.

"I'm kind of not kidding, actually," Calla tells her. "I'm really sorry about everything, and I've totally missed you since . . ."

"Since you stole my boyfriend and faked a date with him to homecoming?"

"It wasn't like that, I didn't—"

"Gotcha." Evangeline pokes her in the arm. "I know he wasn't my boyfriend. He never will be. He's not into me, it's obvious. I guess I just wanted to pretend there was a chance, you know? And you totally ruined my delusional fantasy romance. I so hate when that happens."

Calla laughs. Hard. Then she impulsively hugs Evangeline. Hard. "You're a good friend."

"So are you."

"Really? Even though I ruined your delusional fantasy romance?"

"Happens to the best of us."

They walk on.

Calla watches a phantom stagecoach pass them on the road, with a filmy driver wearing a top hat and a female passenger in a frilly bonnet.

Turning her head, she sees a Native American maiden with an infant in her arms watching from a thicket of lakeside cattails.

Tune out.

She focuses on Evangeline again, telling her, "I just want you to know that I really am sorry."

"Thanks. I'm sorry, too, for acting like such a jerk about the whole thing. Do you forgive me?"

"Are you kidding? Of course."

"Good. You know, the whole time you were away, I wanted to call you and tell you that. Plus, I was kind of worried about you."

"You were? Why?"

"I don't know. I just had this feeling . . . you know? Like something might be wrong. So I was really glad to see you yesterday and hear that the trip was fine."

Far from it, but before Calla can tell her that, Evangeline asks, "So, are you and Jacy . . . ?"

"We're really good friends."

"Oh, please. That's what celebrities tell nosy reporters when they're madly in love with someone who's married or their kids' nanny or thirty years older and filthy rich."

Calla can't help but laugh at that. "Jacy is none of those things."

"Yeah, but you two are more than friends. I've seen him looking at you, and you said he kissed you."

"Okay, we are more than friends. But only if it's okay with you."

Why did I say that? Calla wonders as soon as it's out. Is she really prepared to sacrifice her relationship with Jacy on Evangeline's say-so?

"Well, it's not okay with me."

Great. Here they go again. Now what?

"Gotcha!" Evangeline pokes her in the arm again. "God, you're gullible."

Calla grins, relieved. "Good, because I have to say . . ."

"What? You're head over heels with Jacy and wouldn't give him up just because I asked you to?"

"That, and it seemed like you and Russell were into each other yesterday, so I don't know why you would."

"Oh, Russell. Yeah."

"Evangeline, are you blushing?"

"No."

"Yes. You are. Your face is like a tomato. What's up with Russell? Tell me everything!"

"Got an hour?" Evangeline sighs. "It's kind of a long story."

That's fine with Calla.

Because she has one that's undoubtedly even longer, but she's not in the mood to share it—not even with one of her closest friends.

"Before I tell you about me and Russell," Evangeline says, "I have to ask . . . what do you think about your dad and my aunt getting together?"

"If they do, then I just hope nobody gets hurt."

"Well, I hope the same thing, but . . . they already are."

"Hurt?"

"Together."

Calla raises her eyebrows. "What do you mean?"

"Last night after I went to bed, I realized I forgot something downstairs, and when I came down, I saw them kissing. They didn't see me, so I snuck back up."

"They were kissing?" Calla tries to digest that, but it isn't easy.

Dad kissing a woman who isn't Mom.

Then again . . . did she ever see Dad kissing Mom?

Not in a long, long time.

"I wasn't sure if I should tell you. I don't want to freak you out or anything." Evangeline pauses. "Are you freaked out?"

"Pretty much. Aren't you?"

"Heck, yeah. But, I mean, your dad is so great, and my aunt has been so lonely, and she's stuck with us. . . . I can't help thinking that it would be nice for both of them to have someone. Don't you think?"

"I guess . . ."

"And the other thing is, if your dad falls in love with my

aunt, he'll never want to leave Lily Dale, and you won't have to, either."

Calla can't help but smile. Not because she's thrilled about her dad and Ramona—because she isn't sure how she feels about that—but because her friendship with Evangeline is definitely back on solid ground.

"It wouldn't be the same here without you, Calla."

"I was just thinking the same thing about you," she says, and together, they continue on to school on this beautiful morning after the storm.

EIGHT

Lily Dale
Tuesday, October 9
3:32 p.m.

Evangeline had to stay after school for extra help in English, and Jacy had to run with the track team, so Calla walks home by herself beneath a gloriously blue, sunny sky. It must be eighty-five degrees out.

Everyone at Lily Dale High was buzzing about the weather today, even the teachers. Last year at this time, the area was in the midst of its first snowfall.

Calla—who has never seen snow and is looking forward to it—kept her disappointment to herself. She figures it will arrive soon enough, and when it does, it's notorious for sticking around through late spring.

"Calla! You're back!"

She looks up to see Paula Drumm waving from the front-porch steps of a gray two-story mansard-roofed cottage with scalloped shingles and green trim. A pair of crutches are propped beside her, and her right ankle—which she broke tripping over her sons' toys—is outstretched and wrapped in a bandage.

"Hi, Paula! Hi, boys!" she adds, spotting Dylan and Ethan poking little plastic shovels into the grass near the porch. Above their heads is a shingle that reads MARTIN DRUMM, CLAIRVOYANT. The yard, like so many others in the Dale, is crammed with fall-blooming flowers and lawn decorations ranging from garden gnomes to weathervanes.

"Calla! Want to help us dig to China?" Dylan shouts, lifting his white-blond head.

"China!" little Ethan echoes.

She smiles. "Not today, guys. Some other time, though."

"I heard your dad came back with you," Paula calls, shifting her heavyset frame to lean forward, "and he's living in the Taggarts' guest room."

Still unaccustomed to small-town living, Calla nods. "News travels fast around here."

"You know it."

Yes, she sure does.

She wonders if the Lily Dale gossip mill is already speculating about a romance between Dad and Ramona. If they aren't, they will be.

"I heard something else, too." Paula beckons her closer.

Just like I thought. Calla sighs inwardly and crosses to the front steps, pausing on the way to hug the boys and inspect their hole to China.

"Looks like you'll be there pretty soon," she solemnly tells them.

Dylan nods. "Maybe not in time, though."

"In time for what?

"In time to help."

Something in his expression sends a chill through Calla. She crouches beside him. "What are you going to help with, Dylan?"

"I have to help all the people. They're going to get hurt when all the buildings crash down."

Shuddering inwardly, Calla says, "You're just pretending, right, Dylan? You're just playing superhero again, right?"

He hesitates. Then he nods. "Right!"

"Right!" Ethan agrees, bobbing his blond curls emphatically.

Calla stands, brushes the dirt off her legs, and goes over to Paula.

"They're so cute," she says.

"Yeah, they are. So, Calla, listen, a couple of detectives came to see Patsy Metcalf a little while ago."

Caught off guard, Calla manages to say only, "Um . . . really?"

Already? is what she should have said.

"I heard they were from Florida."

Lutz and Kearney. Wow. She'd known it was coming, but somehow, she had put it out of her mind.

Calla feels like sinking onto the step beside Paula, but she doesn't dare. She doesn't trust herself not to spill the whole story—and in a town like this, that would be a big mistake.

"I heard it had something to do with you," Paula says, "and I wanted to make sure everything is okay."

She's not being nosy—just concerned. And Calla can hardly blame her. After all, she's Paula's children's babysitter. If Paula suspects she's in some kind of trouble with the law, Calla can kiss her part-time income good-bye.

"It's kind of complicated," she tells Paula, "but it's about this woman who broke into my father's house back in Tampa over the weekend."

"Really?"

Paula seems to be waiting for her to elaborate.

When she doesn't, Paula asks, "What does Patsy have to do with it?"

Calla weighs the truth and quickly decides to offer a version of it. "Someone in Patsy's Saturday class had a vision involving the woman, and I mentioned that to the police. I guess they want to check it out."

"Oh, I see." That seems to make perfect sense to Paula, who looks relieved. "Well, I'm glad it wasn't anything serious."

Calla forces a smile. "Like me being wanted for bank robbery or something?"

"Exactly." Paula chuckles. "So, listen, now that we know you're not a wanted felon, can you come babysit tomorrow after school? The boys have been asking for you."

Calla hesitates.

The last time she was there, Dylan drew a picture of her scribbled over in blue crayon and calmly informed her she was under water. And a few weeks ago, he correctly foretold that a man with "a raccoon eye" was trying to hurt her.

"Sure," she tells Paula.

After all, she can't be afraid of a five-year-old. Even one who specializes in making dire predictions—involving Calla— between Candyland moves and story time.

Calla arrives home to find her grandmother in the front yard.

No surprise there.

In Lily Dale, when the weather turns nice, people rush outside to enjoy it from their porches, yards, and gardens.

Odelia—who frequently says her skin is fairer than a baby's keister—is on her knees in a flowerbed, wearing a big, floppy *Little House on the Prairie*-style sunbonnet, enormous aviator sunglasses, and a patch of protective white zinc on her nose.

"Calla! Is it three thirty already? How was school?"

"Same as usual." Calla dumps her heavy backpack on the steps, then sinks down beside it. She plops her chin in her hands and wonders whether to tell her grandmother about the Florida investigators talking to Patsy.

For all she knows, Odelia has already heard.

If she hasn't, she will soon enough. No need to bring it up now.

"Same as usual," Odelia echoes. "Sounds like that's a bad thing?"

"Actually, it isn't." On the contrary, it was comforting to go through a predictable school day after a weekend that was anything but.

"Then why do you look so depressed?"

"Because I stink at math, and I had it last period. Mr. Bombeck hates me."

"I'm sure he doesn't."

"Oh, I'm sure he does. He wasn't exactly loving when he handed back my test." She sighs and leans both elbows back against the top step, legs outstretched to the bottom. "What are you doing, Gammy?"

"Dividing my hostas. Want to help?"

"Dividing?" She groans. "No more math today. Sorry."

Odelia laughs. "It can't be that bad."

"I got a D."

"Minus?"

"No. Just a D."

"Look on the bright side. That's better than a D minus. Or an F." Her grandmother hacks away at a stubborn root.

"Somehow, I don't think the college admissions boards are going to see it that way. My father won't, either. I guess I'd better go tell him." She hoists herself off the step, picks up her backpack, and starts to head inside.

"Calla? If you're going to go tell your father anything right now, you're going to need a boat."

"Why? Where is he?"

"Out on the lake." She gestures vaguely at the patch of blue at the end of the road.

"What?"

"He's fishing . . ."

"He doesn't fish!"

". . . with Ramona." Odelia looks her squarely in the eye as if to ask, *What do you think about that?* "They took a picnic lunch and a lot of bait."

"Oh. Well, that's nice."

"Mmm-hmm." Her grandmother continues to watch her.

"What, Gammy?"

"Are you okay with . . ." She sweeps a dirty gardening glove–covered hand toward the Taggarts' house, "all of this?"

"You mean Dad sleeping in their guest room?" *And the whole town buzzing about it?*

"That. And him maybe . . . starting to move on."

"Are *you*?"

"Why wouldn't I be?"

"I don't know. . . . She was your daughter."

"She was your mother. And his wife." Gammy shrugs. "I'm fine with it. He's gone through hell. He's in a better place than he has been in a long, long time."

"I know. . . . It's been three months."

"Since your mother died."

"What else would I be talking about?"

Her grandmother shakes her head and goes back to chopping the hosta's root.

"Gammy . . . did something happen to my father before my mother died?"

"You tell me."

She knows, Calla realizes. *She knows what Mom did. To Dad. With Darrin.*

"You mean . . . the affair?"

Her grandmother goes still, then sets aside her trowel and looks up at her. "So I was right."

"You mean you didn't know for sure?"

She shakes her head. "My guides were showing me things . . . but I guess I didn't want to believe them."

"What did they show you?" Calla asks, still not certain her grandmother knows it was Darrin.

"The details aren't important."

"Did they show you who my mother was with?"

"It wasn't even that specific. I just got that there was another man, and secrets . . . and guilt. Terrible guilt, on her part."

"Not enough to keep her faithful to Dad, though."

"You don't know that for sure."

"Yes, I do."

When Dad was visiting Lily Dale back in September, he told Calla that for months before she died, Mom had become increasingly detached from him, more absorbed than usual in her work.

Yeah, right. She wasn't traveling on business. She was having an affair.

"It was Darrin Yates, wasn't it," her grandmother says grimly.

"I thought you said your guides didn't show you the details."

"No, but you told me that you'd seen him at the house back in March, and at the funeral. He was obviously back in her life."

"Do you think Dad knew, Gammy?"

"About Darrin?"

"Or just . . . that she was in love with someone else?"

"I doubt Stephanie would spell it out for him, but if that was the case, I'm sure he sensed something was going on. You don't have to be a psychic to know when things aren't right in a marriage."

She's speaking from experience, Calla knows. She can't see Odelia's eyes, but her voice is taut with pain.

"My father told me things weren't the same lately," Calla

tells her. "He told me that my mother had taken a big step back from him before she died. Maybe it was more than that. Maybe he just didn't want me to know the whole story."

"I'm sure he didn't. If *he* even knew the whole story."

Calla shakes her head sadly, feeling terribly sorry for her father . . . and for herself.

"I really thought she loved him."

"Honey, she did. She loved him more than anything—they were good together. When they were first married, when you were born, when you were little . . . the last time I saw them . . . they were crazy about each other. I couldn't imagine that would ever change, but . . . things do. People do."

Feeling sick inside, Calla sinks onto the steps again. "I know people change, but . . . that much?"

"That much."

Calla thinks about Kevin. He changed. Drastically. He went away to college and six months later, broke up with Calla.

Remembering the numbing pain, Calla can't imagine what it would have been like if they had been together for years, were married, with a child.

Poor Dad.

"You know, Calla, your grandfather and I . . . there was a time when we were in love the same way your mother and father were." Her grandmother dusts off her jeans—which are rolled up to reveal her purple socks and orange gardening clogs—and sits beside her. "But then, right around the time I had your mother, Aunt Katie passed away and left the house to me. So Jack and I came here."

Calla looks up at it in surprise—just in time to see a face in the second-story window, looking out at her. Not Miriam's.

This time, it's an old woman with pince-nez glasses and a jet black bun.

"You mean, you didn't always live here?"

"In Lily Dale? No, I used to visit my aunt and my grandmother here in the summers. I always loved it—it felt like home. And when Aunt Katie died, Jack and I were living down near Pittsburgh, and I was pregnant and he was out of work, so we moved in. It wasn't supposed to be permanent."

"Kind of like with me."

Odelia smiles. "Kind of. When I got here, I really began to discover who I was."

"You mean . . . that you were a psychic. And could see the dead. And . . . all that."

"That's what I mean. Sound familiar?"

Calla nods. "Were you seeing spirits, then?"

"Yes. Especially Aunt Katie's."

"Did she have dark, dark hair and wear it in a bun?"

Odelia smiles fondly. "You've seen pictures?"

"I've seen her." Only in Lily Dale would an admission like that not raise an eyebrow.

"Here?" Gammy looks surprised.

"In the window. Just now."

"Really? She doesn't come around all that often anymore. I miss her. I loved our little visits."

Only in Lily Dale, Calla can't help thinking again.

Only in Lily Dale do people speak of spirits dropping in the way they might mention a friend coming for tea.

"Anyway," her grandmother goes on with her tale, "Jack and I settled in here with the baby, and he found work at the steel plant down in Dunkirk. It wasn't long before I really found my calling—I discovered who I was and what I could do, and eventually, I accepted myself. Which is right about the time Jack also discovered who I was—and did the opposite."

"Rejected you?"

"Yes. He just couldn't take it—the spiritualism, and everything that went with it. He thought I was nuts—even when things happened, things he witnessed with his own eyes. Who knows? Maybe he thought *he* was nuts, too. Maybe when he left us, he checked himself into an asylum somewhere."

"You mean he just . . . took off?"

"In the middle of the night. Yup. Left a note that said *You're better off this way.* That was it. I thought the note was meant for Stephanie . . . but I guess it was for both of us. He left both of us. Your mother was too young to remember, thank God."

"She never talked about it. Or him."

"No. She never did. I was always worried that it damaged her somehow. And frankly, I was shocked that he left the way he did. Not just me—left her. Whatever happened between the two of us, he loved that child. Doted on her from the moment she was born. She looked just like him, and had so many of his mannerisms. He liked to say she was a chip off the old block. I guess I'm just lucky he didn't take her with him when he disappeared."

"You never heard from him again?"

"Nope." She shrugs, takes off her sunglasses, wipes them—and then her eyes—on the hem of her denim shirt.

"Are you okay, Gammy?" Calla touches her shoulder.

"Sure. It's been a long time, you know. A lifetime. And this sort of thing does happen around here. Believe me, Jack's not the first person to ever take off and not look back."

Thinking of Darrin—and of her friend Blue Slayton's mother—Calla nods slowly. "Why do they leave, do you think?"

"Jack left because he was weak. Plain and simple. I can't speak for anyone else. Actually, I probably shouldn't even be speaking for Jack . . . but . . . well, I knew him. I knew why he left."

"What do you think ever happened to him?"

"Oh, he's back in Pittsburgh. Remarried, with grown kids and grandkids. Still a steelworker, after all these years."

"How do you know that?"

Odelia raises an eyebrow at her. "Let's put it this way. If someone like me really wants to find someone . . . they can usually be found. *Capisce?*"

Calla nods slowly. *"Capisce."*

If someone like me really wants to find someone . . . they can usually be found.

Someone like Odelia, Calla thinks. . . .

And someone like me.

Upstairs in her room, Calla types in her mother's e-mail password.

L-E-O-L-Y-N.

Her hand trembling on the key, she hits Enter, then waits for the mail files to load.

It doesn't take long.

Her breath seems deafening in her own ears as she scrolls up through the archives, back to last winter.

She forces herself to reread the first exchange between her mother and Darrin, when they were rediscovering each other after all those years, and making secret plans to meet in Boston.

Then she opens the first contact that came after. The one she couldn't go on reading the other day.

> Darrin (like I told you, I can never call you Tom, no matter what you want me to do, sorry!)—seeing you yesterday was incredible, despite everything. You said you wanted me to think about what you told me, about what happened back then, and I've done nothing but that since you left me at the airport. A part of me can't believe it really even happened, but I know you wouldn't lie. Yes, you made some mistakes—terrible mistakes—but I understand why you did what you did. You were a kid, and afraid, and you thought you were doing what was best for me, and for you, and for our child.

That was where Calla left off before.

Now, she takes a deep breath and keeps reading.

> Do you remember what a nightmare it was, the two of us alone in Leolyn Woods, with me giving birth to a baby no one even knew we were expecting? Sometimes I can't believe it really happened. I was scared out of my mind. I was in so much pain that I couldn't think straight. I don't remember much of it, other than when you told me the baby hadn't made it.

Calla gasps and covers her mouth with her hand.

The baby hadn't made it.

Oh, no. Please, no.

She rereads the lines again, and then again, just to be sure.

Her eyes fill with tears for the loss of a sister or brother she had never even known.

And now I never will.

I told you I was devastated, and I really was—but there was a part of me that might have been a tiny bit relieved, too. I've never forgiven myself for that. How could I feel that way? How could I be so selfish? Now that I'm a mother, I question that every day of my life. If anything ever happened to my daughter, I wouldn't want to live. I would give my life for her. Yet there was a time when I was secretly grateful that I wouldn't have to be a mother.

All I could think was that no one would ever have to know. We could go back to our normal lives. We had managed to hide it all those months, but I knew once the baby came, the whole town would be talking. Now no one would ever even know I had been pregnant.

But we didn't get back to normal. When you left, Darrin, my life was over. How could you just disappear?

I know you want to tell me all about it. Maybe I should have let you keep talking the other night, but I just couldn't hear any more. Even now, I look into my heart for a way to forgive you. The only way I can do that is to forgive myself, too, for the relief I felt when you told me our baby had died.

I don't know if I can forgive myself. I know I can never forget. Even now. Every day, when I lived in Lily Dale, I looked out at that lake and remembered what you had done. I kept picturing you wrapping our dead baby in a blanket and weighing it down with rocks and tossing it into the water. You said you did it to protect me, and I believed that—until you left. Then I felt like you had done it to protect only yourself. I knew I had to leave Lily Dale. I felt like everyone in town knew what had happened, like they were all looking at me.

I have to end this here. My daughter just came home from school. I hear her downstairs. I'll talk to you soon. I do love you. And I will try to forgive you.

Stephanie

Through eyes blurred with tears, Calla reads the e-mail again, and again, and again.

Then she closes the screen.

That's enough for today.

Maybe it's enough, period.

Now she knows why her mother left Lily Dale and never looked back.

Now her dream—or memory—of the argument between Mom and Odelia makes sense.

The only way to know for sure is to dredge the lake.

That's what they were talking about. Dredging the lake to look for the baby's remains.

Calla shudders.

So.

Her grandmother knew about the baby.

When—and how—did she find out?

Why didn't she tell Calla? She's had plenty of opportunities.

Well, she can't stay silent about it forever.

I won't let her, Calla thinks, jaw set with grim determination.

NINE

Lily Dale
Tuesday, October 9
7:28 p.m.

"What's the matter, Calla?"

She looks up from her mashed potatoes—artfully arranged around the edges of her plate, the better to hide the fact that she's not eating them—to see both her father and grandmother watching her across the kitchen table.

"Nothing," she lies, and cuts off a tiny chunk of meatloaf with her fork. She pops it into her mouth, chews, and smiles brightly.

See? I'm not quietly freaking out about my dead sibling being dumped into the lake that's right outside the doorstep.

Obviously not fooled, her grandmother presses a hand to her forehead. "You don't have a fever."

"I'm not sick, Gammy."

"You don't have to have a fever to be sick." Dad, his face tinted bright pink from his afternoon on the lake, looks concerned. "You haven't said two words since we sat down."

"I know." She puts down her fork, giving up the charade. "I'm just . . . worried. You know. About math."

A knowing gleam enters Odelia's eyes behind her pink-framed glasses. She says nothing, going back to her own mashed potatoes and meatloaf.

"What about math?"

"I got a D on a test," she tells her father, and it's his turn to look sick.

"I don't blame you for being worried. That's not good."

"No kidding."

"After dinner," he says, "you and I are going to work on math together."

"Actually, Dad, I already have a study partner. Willow York is helping me."

"You can never have too many study partners."

"Dad, you don't have to—"

"What else have I got to do?" He spears a green bean with his fork.

"I don't know . . . isn't Ramona waiting for you to get back over there?"

Dad looks up from his plate. "Does it bother you?"

Odelia, conspicuously silent, pours herself more cream soda.

"Does what bother me?"

"That I'm staying next door with Ramona?"

"No, it's fine."

He doesn't look convinced. "Does it bother you that we . . . went fishing today?"

"Why would it?"

"I don't know. Maybe it would. And that would be understandable, because—"

"Knock-knock," a voice calls through the open screen at the front door.

Ramona.

The three of them look at one another.

It's Odelia who calls, "Come on in!"

Moments later, Ramona enters the kitchen, carrying a loaf of banana bread. "I thought you might want this for dessert. I always make two."

"That's sweet of you. Thank you, Ramona." Odelia takes it from her and carries it over to the counter. "Have a seat. Did you eat dinner?"

"The kids and I had wings. I don't want to interrupt, so I'll just—"

"No, stay," Dad says, and pulls out the empty chair between his and Calla's.

"Are you sure?"

"Sit down, Ramona." Odelia opens a cupboard door. "I'm making coffee."

Ramona looks at Calla. "How are you, sweetie?"

"I'm great," she lies. "Thanks for bringing the banana bread."

As if that's all the encouragement she needs, Ramona settles into a chair with a jangle of gypsy jewelry.

She's dressed slightly more conservatively than usual, though, Calla notices. Instead of one of her flowing dresses or skirts, she's wearing jeans and a T-shirt—although it's a tie-dye one. She's got makeup on.

Dad is obviously really glad to see her. He looks happy all of a sudden. Happy like Calla hasn't seen him in a long, long time.

Calla can't help but forgive him for kissing Ramona. After all they've been through, he does deserve happiness—maybe someone to lean on now and then.

Suddenly, she wants—needs—to talk to Jacy. She pushes back her chair. "I'm going up to my room. Good night, everyone."

"What about the banana bread?" her grandmother asks. "And I was thinking we could play cards."

"I've really got a lot of homework to do, Gammy."

"Now that's dedicated." Ramona gives an approving nod. "That'll be the day when Evangeline passes up dessert to study. She's only home right now because I made her stay and finish her social studies project that's due in the morning."

"I'll come and help you with your math," her father offers, looking about as reluctant to skip dessert with Ramona as Calla is to have him come upstairs with her.

"I've got to write an essay for English, Dad, actually. We can work on math tomorrow."

"Are you sure?"

"Positive."

She really does have an essay to write.

Upstairs, she dials Jacy's number.

Walt, one of his foster dads, answers the phone.

"Calla, how's it going?"

"Pretty good. Is Jacy there?"

"No, Peter took him to get something to eat after track, and then they were going to go try to buy posterboard somewhere for a social studies project he has due tomorrow but has apparently known about for a week. Nothing like waiting till the last minute, huh?"

Calla, who had the same project but finished it before she left for Florida, isn't quite sure what to say to that, other than, "Can you please ask him to call me when he gets back?"

"Sweetie, I'll tell him you called, but when he gets back he's got to work on his project, and I have a feeling he's not going to be done until midnight. So if it's not an emergency . . . ?"

"No," Calla admits, "it's not. I just wanted"—more like *desperately needed*—"to talk to him. But it can wait till school tomorrow."

She hangs up, considers calling Evangeline, and decides against it. Ramona mentioned that she, too, is working on her project. And anyway, Calla does have that English essay to write.

But it takes her several hours to get anything down, and she's pretty sure, when she turns off the light and climbs into bed, that it doesn't make much sense.

Nothing makes sense.

What her mother and Darrin did wasn't just immoral. It was illegal.

Was that why Mom and Odelia argued over it?

And . . .

Was there really any doubt whether Darrin actually dumped the baby into the lake?

She keeps remembering the spot Aiyana led her to a few

weeks ago, in Leolyn Woods. Lilies of the valley were inexplicably blooming there. In October.

And there was a rock, standing upright.

Like an unmarked tombstone.

"She isn't there," Aiyana said cryptically when Calla found it.

At the time, she had no idea what her spirit guide meant.

Now, though, she wonders.

She wonders about a lot of things.

Lying in bed, the lace curtains billowing lightly at the open window, she hears the screen door creak below.

Ramona and her father call good night to Odelia.

"Thanks for the banana bread. See you two tomorrow."

You two.

As if they're a couple.

Maybe they aren't yet.

But they will be, Calla acknowledges as the sound of their laughter floats up through the window.

TEN

Lily Dale
Wednesday, October 10
12:53 p.m.

As always, Calla keeps an eye out for Jacy as she goes through the cafeteria line.

She needs to tell him what she learned yesterday. About Mom and Darrin . . . and their dead baby.

The baby they hid in the murky bottom of Cassadaga Lake.

No wonder her grandmother didn't want Calla to set foot in that water. The warning had nothing to do with any premonition about Sharon Logan trying to drown her.

No wonder she and Mom were talking about dredging the lake.

They were talking about finding the baby's remains there.

Why, though?

Was there any doubt about the child's final resting place?

Calla can't stop thinking about the little grave Aiyana showed her in the woods just last week, in a spot where lilies of the valley was somehow blooming at the wrong time of year.

Jacy . . . where are you?

Calla dumps chickpeas on her salad and scans the big, crowded room.

No sign of him.

They share the same lunch period, but Jacy often skips it in favor of slipping out of school for a while. Of course, that's against the rules, but he doesn't seem to care.

"Sometimes, I just need to get outdoors and breathe," he told Calla when she asked him why he's willing to risk getting caught and being assigned to in-school detention . . . not that he ever has been.

Yesterday, she skipped with him after finding a note stuck in the vents at the top of her locker door:

Meet me for lunch.

She didn't have to ask where.

He'd brought them a couple of peanut butter sandwiches. They ate them sitting on a fallen log in the overgrown thicket behind the school. Jacy fed most of his to a chipmunk that came over and actually ate out of his hand.

"You're like Snow White or something," Calla had told him with a grin.

"Snow White?" He'd raised a dark eyebrow at her. "Snow White?"

"You know, she was always surrounded by forest creatures."

"So was Tarzan. And he was a lot more manly than Snow White," Jacy had said, and they laughed.

Jacy has always seemed most comfortable in the great outdoors, moving through the woods as easily as most people walk through their own living room.

But when he's sitting across the aisle from Calla in math class, he always seems restless in his seat, and sometimes she catches him staring longingly out the window.

Now, as she pays the cashier and carries her tray toward her usual table, she concludes that he's not in the cafeteria today. Why would he be?

Indian summer has definitely settled over Lily Dale.

Again this morning, Calla awoke to find the sun shining; again, she left her coat behind.

And again, her father was lounging on the Taggarts' front porch with a cup of coffee—and Ramona—when she headed off to school.

It was nice to see him there . . . sort of.

But Calla is starting to wonder if she'd rather he stayed at Odelia's, despite the close quarters. It's kind of strange to have him around . . . but not around.

This morning when she and Evangeline were walking to school together, Calla almost asked her friend again what she thought about all of this.

But Evangeline had a lot to say.

Most of it about Russell Lancione.

They'd talked on the phone for over an hour last night while she was supposed to be working on her project—which she wound up throwing together at the last minute, before her aunt got home. He'd asked her to study together again tonight, and Evangeline was starting to *like him*—like him.

Which was great for her, and great for Russell, and great for Calla, too—not just because she wants her friend to be happy, but because it takes some of the pressure off her dating Jacy.

Still, Evangeline in love—or, okay, just in *like*-like—is even more talkative than the usual Evangeline. Who could be pretty talkative.

Calla has barely gotten a word in edgewise since they made up.

That's probably a good thing, because what if Calla were to mention her mother's secret past to Evangeline and Evangeline slipped and told her aunt and her aunt went and told Dad, or he even just happened to overhear?

That would not be good.

So far, the only ones who know there even was a baby are Jacy and Odelia. And Jacy's definitely not talkative under any circumstances, so it's safe with him.

Right, so it's better this way—Evangeline wrapped up in Russell, and not asking too many questions about what happened in Florida. All she knows so far is that a woman broke into the Delaneys' house there and attacked Calla.

That's more than her friends Willow York and Sarita Abernathie know.

But now, when she deposits her lunch tray on their usual table and starts to sit down, she can't help but notice that they suddenly stop talking.

Exactly the way people do when the person they're talking about suddenly appears.

Back when she first met beautiful, brainy Willow—who happens to be a recent ex-girlfriend of Blue Slayton—Calla mistook her reserved nature for standoffishness. Then Mr. Bombeck assigned her as Calla's math study partner, and she found an unexpected friend in Willow—and her lovable, ailing mom, Althea.

"Hi, Calla," Sarita says as she sits down.

Willow says nothing at all. Which is unusual.

"What's up?" Calla unwraps her fork, trying to sound casual, wondering if Willow has suddenly had a change of heart about Blue or something.

That would be fine with Calla. Whatever was going on between her and Blue came to an end the night before homecoming, when Jacy kissed her for the first time.

Or maybe it's not about Blue.

Maybe they, too, have heard about the Florida detectives who came to see Patsy Metcalf yesterday.

"Nothing's up, just . . ." Sarita flashes a mouthful of metal in a smile that doesn't quite reach her eyes. "You know. The usual stuff. Right, Willow?"

She shoots a look at Willow, who, Calla notices, seems awfully interested in removing the label from her water bottle. "Right." Her straight dark hair falls across her face like a curtain.

"Like what stuff?"

"You know . . . school stuff." Sarita gives Calla such an exaggerated shrug that the long earrings dangling beneath her sleek short haircut come to rest horizontally on her shoulders.

"What kind of school stuff?"

"For one thing, the board of education is trying to take

away our right to have bake-sale fundraisers. Did you hear?"

"No." And Calla's pretty sure that that's *not* what Sarita and Willow were just talking about.

"Well, it's true. I'm going to start a petition. But not today, because I have a major social studies test tomorrow afternoon and my parents will kill me if I don't get at least an A."

"At least?"

"You know my parents."

Yeah. Calla does know Sarita's parents. They head a family of overachievers, albeit "mere mortals," who live outside Lily Dale's gates. Sarita's brother is in medical school, her sister is a sophomore at Yale, and Sarita is hell-bent on going Ivy, too.

"That reminds me," Calla says. "Did either of you finish making your lists of reach schools, target schools, and safety schools for Mrs. Erskine? Because I have to meet with her tomorrow."

"I did that last week," Sarita says, "but right now I feel like my safety schools are reach schools unless I get my act together."

"Yeah . . . same here," Calla says.

Willow looks up at last. She's as model-gorgeous as ever, but Calla is startled to see that her dark eyes are rimmed with red, as if she's been crying. "Calla, did your dad freak about your math grade?"

"Not really. He pretty much just said I need to work harder on it."

"That's it?" Willow asks. "You thought he was going to make a big deal about it."

"I know. Luckily he didn't." She wonders whether to mention Ramona popping over in the midst of the discussion, and decides not to. "He just said he's going to help me study now that he's around."

"Is that a good thing," Sarita asks, "or a bad thing?"

"Are you kidding? I can use all the help I can get. Between Willow and my dad, I might be able to not fail the next test."

"About that . . ." Willow trails off and looks at Sarita, who gives a slight nod.

"I'm going to go to the library and start studying," Sarita announces, pushing her chair back. "I'll see you guys later."

Uh-oh. Something's up.

Willow gets right to the point. "I don't think I'm going to be able to help you this week, really. My, um, my mom . . . she's in the hospital."

Oh.

Oh, no.

I should have known.

From the moment Calla met Althea York, she had sensed that the woman was ill.

"What happened?" she asks, trying not to betray the tide of dread sweeping through her.

Maybe she was wrong. Maybe Althea slipped and fell and broke her arm or something.

"Cancer. She was getting chemo but the treatments stopped working last summer."

Calla feels as though someone just hit her in the stomach with a two-by-four.

"But . . . I mean, there are so many new drugs, aren't there? I thought—"

"No, it's too late for her." Willow holds her head stoically high. "She doesn't have much time left. The doctors say there's nothing else they can do."

"Oh, Willow . . ."

"You and Sarita are the only ones who know."

"Oh, Willow . . ." Without stopping to think, Calla throws her arms around her friend. "I'm so sorry."

Willow's thin frame is shaking violently, and Calla feels her tears dampening her own shoulder.

Somehow, all around them, the usual cafeteria chaos continues. Nobody is aware of Willow's tragedy.

But I know. I know what it's like to lose your mother.

Calla, too, is crying.

"What am I going to do?" Willow pulls back and wipes her face with a napkin Calla hands her. "How can I live without her?"

"You can."

"No." Willow sobs into the napkin. "I can't."

"You can. You will."

"No . . ."

Calla grips both of Willow's bony shoulders. "Look at me. Please."

Willow looks at her, desolate. Her face is ravaged with a pain that's all too familiar to Calla.

"You'll go on. You'll live without her. You have to. I mean, think about it. What's the alternative?"

"I'm so afraid."

"I know. It's awful. It's so awful, and hard and unfair, but . . . you'll survive. I promise. Listen, if I can, you can." She grabs her friend's hand and squeezes it. "I'll help you get through it."

"I don't want to be alone."

Her voice is so small. So frightened. So familiar.

"You aren't alone, Willow."

"I really am, without her. But I don't turn eighteen until January. What am I supposed to do until then? Go live with my father and his new wife and ruin their perfect new family?"

"He just lives down in Dunkirk, right? That's only a few miles away. You could still—"

"No. He doesn't want me."

"Sure, he does."

"No. He's not like your father. Do you know what he said when I called him last night and asked if he could meet me at the hospital because Mom had just been rushed there in an ambulance?"

"What?"

"He said that he'd see what he could do, because he and his wife had to go to open house at his daughter's school. He'd see what he could do," she repeats, shaking her head in disgust.

"Did he show up?"

"Yeah, for, like, two minutes. Then he asked me what time I thought I'd be done there, because if I was going to sleep at his house, they wouldn't have to get a babysitter after all while they were at open house."

"So . . . did you stay there? And babysit?"

"No. I stayed in the hospital."

Calla swallows a lump in her throat, picturing Willow curled up in a hospital bed in the middle of the night, beside her dying mother.

"How did you get back here?"

"I have my mom's car. I'm going back there after school, too. I'm staying tonight, and every night until . . ."

She can't say it.

"Willow . . ." Calla can't say it, either. "Listen, you can't move into the hospital. That's . . ."

What? Crazy? Unhealthy? Heartbreaking?

"I can't leave her. And I'm not going to stay at my father's," she adds defiantly, "or . . . home. Alone."

"You can come stay with me and my grandmother."

"Yesterday you said that your dad has to stay next door because you don't have any room."

"I meant for him. You can stay in my room, with me. My grandmother borrowed a cot from Andy when my friend Lisa came to stay, and—"

"That's sweet, Calla." Willow flashes a sad smile. "But I can't leave my mother. I need to be with her."

Her voice breaks, and suddenly, she looks ten years younger. Tears stream down her face again.

"I need my mother. I can't lose her."

Calla has no more words of comfort.

"I know," is all she can say, over and over. "I know."

"Hey, what brings you out here?" Jacy makes room for Calla on the moss-covered fallen log.

"You." She sinks down beside him. "I need you and I figured this was where you'd be."

"I need you, too—but I never thought you'd come out here two days in a row. You don't like to break the rules. Skipping lunch. Kissing guys in the woods when you're supposed to be in school. . . ."

"I'm not—"

"Oh, yeah, you are." He pulls her close and his lips meet hers.

It's tempting—so tempting—for Calla to forget all about everything but Jacy, right here, right now. That would be the easiest, and probably the healthiest, thing to do. It's what she would have done a few months ago, when she was just a normal girl surrounded by others who were just like her, kids with intact families and enough money, kids who didn't know things they couldn't, shouldn't possibly know, about the past or the future or other people's lives in this world or the next.

But Calla is no longer that girl, and she needs to talk to Jacy. Now.

She forces herself to break the kiss, to pull back, out of his embrace, to look away, at the trees, at the overcast sky, at the sparse hint of sun struggling to break through.

She thinks about her friend Althea, dying in a hospital bed. And Willow, who left the cafeteria with tears in her eyes, saying she wanted to be alone for a while. And that poor little baby, lying stiff in a blanket, weighed down with rocks in a watery grave.

"You found out more about your mother."

Startled, she looks up at Jacy. "How did you know?"

He smiles faintly. "A little bird told me. Like Snow White. What's up?"

She tells him. As she talks, he stops eating.

"That's the worst thing I've ever heard," he says when she finishes.

"The worst thing?"

"Okay, maybe not. It would have been worse if . . ."

"If what?" she asks when he trails off, narrowing his eyes.

"You know, if . . . the baby hadn't died of natural causes."

Calla's stomach turns over. "But it did. I mean, it died at birth."

"You know that because . . . ?"

"Because that's what she wrote. That's what Darrin told her."

Jacy remains silent.

"You don't think they killed the baby, do you? Because I know my mother—" Even as the words spill from her lips, Calla wonders how true they are.

She doesn't know her mother. Not anymore.

"I don't think she killed the baby," Jacy says, to her relief.

"You think Darrin did?"

"No. I don't think that, either. I just . . . well, it makes me wonder. We've both seen him, Calla. His spirit. We've both heard him trying to apologize to her. For what?"

"For putting their baby's body in the lake instead of giving it a proper burial."

"Are you sure about that?"

No.

She isn't sure of anything.

"Jacy . . . what if he killed the baby? Do you think that's why he's hanging around? Is he trying to stop me from finding out?"

"I don't know. But you have to be careful. I don't like this."

"I don't, either."

109

"Maybe you should tell someone."

"Like who?"

"You said your grandmother knows about it, right?"

"She must. But I don't know how much."

"I think you need to talk to her, Calla. And the sooner, the better."

"I know."

"The other thing is . . . Walt and Peter told me this morning that a couple of detectives were nosing around town yesterday."

"I heard. They talked to Patsy Metcalf, and I'm sure they're looking for Bob." He's the red-bearded student in her Saturday morning class who had the vision about the purple house in Geneseo.

"They found him, actually. Asked him all kinds of questions. I think it freaked him out a little."

"Maybe I should go talk to him."

"You probably should."

"I don't know where to find him."

"It's not exactly like looking for a needle in a haystack around here. I'm sure you can find him without a whole lot of effort," Jacy points out. Then he adds, "What about the Yateses?"

"What about them?"

"You haven't told them yet. About Darrin. They're getting ready to leave for Arizona for the winter. Don't you think it's time?"

Calla sighs. "I guess it is."

The grim task can't wait forever. It isn't fair to those poor people, growing old without their son, wondering whatever happened to him.

The news is going to break their hearts.

No, it won't, Calla tells herself. *Their hearts are already broken.*

"Will you really go with me?"

Jacy nods. "After school?"

"Yes. No, wait, I can't. I'm babysitting at Paula's till five. How about tomorrow?"

"How about after you babysit? I really don't think this should wait."

He's right.

She sighs. "Okay. I'll meet you by the lake when I'm done babysitting."

"Want to stop home first to drop off your backpack or something?"

"No, let's just get it over with. Although—what about Darrin's obituary? Maybe we should find a place to print it out off the Internet, so we can show his parents in case they don't believe us."

"I already did. I'll bring it with me."

"Why do you have it?"

"After what happened this past weekend . . ." Jacy shrugs. "I figured you might need it. As . . ."

"Evidence?"

"Pretty much. And now that those detectives are in town . . . maybe you should tell them about it, if they show up to talk to you again."

"Do you think they will?"

"Don't you?"

"I guess."

This day just keeps on getting better and better.

"Calla, you can't withhold information from the police. You've got to tell them everything you know."

"But they already have Sharon Logan in custody."

"They need to know she might be responsible for more than one death."

He's right.

She knows he is.

And she can't go on protecting her father forever. Sooner or later, the whole truth is going to come out.

What then?

ELEVEN

All afternoon, as Calla went through the motions of digging to China with Dylan and Ethan—and trying not to be uneasy when Dylan kept talking about saving the hurt people there—her thoughts flew from Althea to the dead baby and back again.

"How come you're not talking to us, Calla?" Dylan asked her at one point, and she made an effort after that.

It was a relief when her duties came to an end—until she allowed herself to remember what's coming next.

Now, as she rounds a bend and sees Jacy waiting for her in the pavilion, her stomach starts to churn.

"Hey," he says, and reaches out to grab both her hands in both of his, pulling her closer. "Are you ready?"

"I feel like I'm going to pass out."

"Is that a no?"

She sighs. "It's a yes. Let's go."

"Here, give me your backpack. I'll carry it."

"That's okay."

"It weighs a ton. Give it to me." He holds out his arm.

She hands over the backpack.

"Better?" he asks as he slings it over his own back.

She nods. Surprisingly, it does feel better to have the literal weight taken off her shoulders. Too bad she can't hand over the figurative one as well.

"Come on." He laces his fingers through hers and gives them a squeeze. "It's going to be okay."

"I'm dreading this."

"I know you are. But you can't keep putting it off. And you're stronger than you know. Look at all you've been through. Most people would crumple up and cry."

"Don't think I haven't," she tells him, but finds herself warmed by his praise.

They walk in silence toward Erie Boulevard, a narrow, rutted road on the far eastern end of town. She tries not to think about their last confrontation with Darrin's parents, who basically let her know that they somehow blamed her mother for their son's disappearance.

Of course, Calla wrongly blamed Darrin for Mom's death, so who is she to hold a grudge?

"Just take a deep breath," Jacy advises as she stops walking, seeing the Yateses' shingle and glassed-in front porch come into view.

"What if they're not home?" she asks hopefully, despite the car parked in the driveway.

"They are."

"I know." She draws a shaky breath into her lungs, holds it, and exhales through puffed cheeks. "Okay, let's go."

As they slowly climb the steps to the white aluminum door, a dog begins barking somewhere inside the house.

At last, Jacy lets go of her fingers with a final squeeze and rings the bell.

The last time they were here, the porch was fixed up like an indoor-outdoor living room, with lamps, a television, and furniture. Now Calla can see through the window that there's nothing but a stretch of bare teal carpet and several cardboard moving boxes stacked near the door.

Clearly, the Yateses are getting ready to vacate their cottage for the winter.

Mr. Yates, a gray-haired, balding man, steps onto the porch, accompanied by a barking terrier. As Darrin's father peers at them through the window in the door, Calla sees a spark of recognition—quickly followed by dismay—in his gray-blue eyes, behind a pair of wire-framed bifocals.

"Jasmine, shh, down, girl." He collars the dog and opens the door a crack. "Yes?"

"Hi, Mr. Yates. I'm not sure if you remember me. . . ." Yes, she is sure he does, but it seems polite to reintroduce herself. "I'm Calla Delaney. Odelia Lauder's granddaughter?"

And Stephanie Lauder Delaney's daughter, but no need to voice that aloud. He knows.

"Hello."

"And this is my . . ." "Friend" seems wrong. And this is not the best moment to call him her boyfriend for the first time. "This is Jacy Bly."

Mr. Yates offers Jacy the same polite, yet frosty, nod.

"I need to speak to you—and your wife, too. It's about your son."

He raises a bushy gray eyebrow. "What about him?"

Calla falters.

"It's probably a good idea if we come inside and sit down," Jacy speaks up. "If you don't mind."

"No. Come in," he says heavily, as if he realizes, somehow, what's coming.

Still keeping a grip on the dog, he leads them into a sparsely decorated living room that's shockingly uncluttered by Lily Dale standards.

"We're getting ready to leave this weekend for Arizona," Mr. Yates explains, sweeping an arm around the room. "Most of our things are packed away. Have a seat. I'll be right back."

He shuts the dog into a room at the back of the house amid barking protests, then goes upstairs.

Calla and Jacy perch close together on an uncomfortable sofa with stiff, shiny green-and-brown-striped fabric.

"Are you okay?" Jacy asks in a low voice, reaching into his pocket.

She nods, afraid her voice will crack if she tries to speak.

She's not okay. She's a nervous wreck.

Especially when she sees Jacy remove a folded sheet of printer paper from his pocket.

What if the Yateses don't believe it? What if they think the article is a fake?

About to ask Jacy what he thinks, she looks up, then does a double take, spotting something over his shoulder.

"Darrin is here," she whispers to Jacy, knowing she probably shouldn't be surprised to see him.

"Where?"

She points to the apparition sitting somewhat stiffly in a chair behind him. "Can you see him?"

"No, but I can feel him," Jacy says simply.

Footsteps creak on the stair treads, and Mr. Yates descends with his wife, a wiry, petite woman with cropped silver hair.

"You remember Calla and Jacy," he says, and she nods, looking about as thrilled to see them in her living room as Calla is to see Darrin.

In silence, the Yateses arrange themselves in a pair of wingback chairs facing the couch.

Then the four of them look at one another for a few awkward moments.

To Calla's surprise, Darrin drifts across the room toward her, and gives a slight nod.

She clears her throat. "Mr. and Mrs. Yates, I don't know how to say this, so . . . I mean, I guess I just have to say it. I know you've been looking for your son for years, and I know you said you both believe he's still alive. . . ."

No, they don't, she realizes, stunned to see the sorrowful expression in both sets of eyes that are fixated on her.

They said they sensed that Darrin was still on the earth plane, and maybe they really did, while he was.

But not anymore.

Something Ramona told Calla a while back comes back to her.

Nothing is more powerful than the bond between a parent and a child, but there are some things a parent might not want to see, or accept.

The Yateses know.

They probably couldn't admit it to her and Jacy, and possibly not even to each other, but they already know their son is dead.

The realization that she's not about to deliver shocking news—and that they probably won't question the newspaper article's validity—makes it a little easier for Calla to go on. Especially when she sees Darrin go stand between their two chairs, resting a hand on both his mother's and his father's shoulders.

"I'm sorry to have to be the one to tell you this," Calla says gently, "but I found an article on the Internet about Darrin—he was living in Maine, under another name—and it says he . . . passed away. A few months ago."

Mr. Yates flinches as though he's been struck by a heavy object and squeezes his eyes closed as if to ward off the pain.

Mrs. Yates lets out a sob and buries her face in her hands.

"I'm so sorry," Calla says again, feeling helpless.

Yes, they knew . . . but it doesn't make hearing it aloud any easier to bear.

Who knows that better than her? She's the one who found her mother at the foot of the stairs. She immediately realized she was dead, but when the paramedics arrived to confirm it, she fell apart all over again.

"I'm sorry for your loss," Jacy tells the Yateses as they embrace each other.

For a few minutes, Mrs. Yates cries inconsolably on her husband's shoulder as, tearful himself, he tries to comfort her. Darrin is beside them, watching sadly yet peacefully.

It's almost as if he's okay with where he is, Calla realizes. He doesn't seem to mind being dead. He just doesn't want his parents to hurt.

After a few minutes, they manage to compose themselves and again face Calla and Jacy, this time with their veiny old hands clasped in the space between the chairs.

"Tell us," Mr. Yates says, "about our son. About what you found."

"It might be easier to show you." Calla looks at Jacy.

He nods and holds out the article from the Internet.

The Yateses lean their heads close together and read it silently. Mrs. Yates is crying again, but her husband seems to have steeled himself against emotion.

"So . . . he was murdered. I guess that should surprise me."

Calla and Jacy look at each other, then back at Mr. Yates.

"It doesn't surprise you?" Calla asks.

He shrugs. "I never had a good feeling about my son. He was such a good little boy. . . ." His voice breaks and he looks down, pulling a handkerchief from his pocket.

"Then he got involved with drugs," Mrs. Yates tells them,

shaking her head. "It happens a lot, to gifted young people who don't want to see the things they can see. Darrin was frightened by his abilities. He tried to shut things out, numb himself. Drugs did that."

Calla nods, sympathizing with the young man who was undoubtedly bombarded with the same things she is—ghostly images and voices, and premonitions you can't do anything about.

For the first time, she grasps the importance of learning how to channel the energy around her, how to tune in and tune out. Not to would put her in danger in more ways than she ever really comprehended.

"I imagine he got himself into some kind of trouble with a drug dealer, or something like that," Mr. Yates comments, gesturing with the article about Darrin's murder.

His wife nods glumly. "I don't want to know the details. Do you?"

Her husband shakes his head. "What does it matter?" He hands the article back to Jacy and stands. So does Mrs. Yates.

Clearly the visit is over. It's time to leave the Yateses to grieve in private. Calla and Jacy get up, too.

"Thank you for telling us," Mrs. Yates says, when they reach the front door.

To Calla's surprise, she reaches out with a thin, bony, deeply veined hand and gives Calla's fingers a squeeze. "I'm truly sorry about your mother."

"Thank you. And I'm so sorry about your son." She hesitates, wondering if she should mention the link between the two murders.

No.

That will come out in time, with the police investigation.

Maybe, she realizes when she gets home, even sooner than she thinks.

"Calla! There you are. Where have you been?" her grand-mother hurries into the front hall the moment she steps over the threshold.

"Babysitting."

"Paula said you left at five. I called over there looking for you."

"Is everything all right?" she asks, suddenly frightened.

"Everything's fine, but—where were you?"

"I ran into Jacy on the way home. Sorry. Why were you looking for me?" she asks, though she wouldn't really blame her grandmother for trying to keep closer tabs on her after the lie she told about the homecoming dance.

"A couple of detectives were just here wanting to talk to you. From Florida. I told them to come back tomorrow after school. I'll make sure I'm here with you, and I'll tell your father, too."

"No, wait, Gammy—I'd rather talk to them without him, okay?"

"I don't think—"

"Please, Gammy. There are some things I have to tell them, and—I just don't want him to hear them just yet."

Odelia sighs. "Okay. But you know it's all going to come out sooner or later."

"I know."

"You can't take on the weight of the world, sweetie. You're just a kid." Her grandmother hugs her, hard.

Calla tries to swallow the ache in her throat.

Just a kid.

When, she wonders, was the last time she felt young and carefree?

And will she ever feel that way again?

T W E L V E

Lily Dale
Wednesday, October 10
7:50 p.m.

"Too bad Odelia couldn't have come with us," Dad comments, pulling the rental car into his usual spot in front of the house after a casual dinner at B.J.'s Downwind Café in Fredonia.

"Yeah, that would have been good," Calla agrees.

It had been a quiet dinner, just the two of them, trying to make conversation while eating Buffalo wings—not that the locals call them that. Around here, as she keeps reminding her father, they're just "wings." Kind of like Lily Dale is just "the Dale."

The stilted meal is what it was like between Calla and her father last summer when Mom first passed away, and they had to figure out how to communicate without her to bridge the conversational gap.

Calla had thought they had that all figured out by now, but for some reason, tonight was . . . awkward.

Maybe it's partly because she's been feeling increasingly preoccupied about Althea York. That tragedy has almost overshadowed her confrontation with the Yateses and the disturbing discovery that she doesn't have a long-lost sibling after all.

Dad has seemed preoccupied all night, too.

Probably thinking about Ramona. He invited her, Evangeline, and Mason to join them for dinner, but they turned down the invitation.

"We had wings last night, and anyway, you two need some father-daughter time," Ramona said with her easy grin. "You don't need the rest of us horning in."

At the time, Calla was grateful.

Now, she wishes someone had tagged along to defuse the silence, even if it would have meant Dad and Ramona mooning all over each other all night.

"Looks like Odelia's not home yet," Dad observes, looking up at the darkened house and empty driveway beside it.

"No, she had an appointment. She probably won't be home until later."

Much later. Her grandmother is conducting a home message circle in Westfield tonight, and those can go till all hours.

"She sure has a lot of appointments, doesn't she?" Dad looks thoughtful.

"Yeah, well . . . she's busy."

"Counseling people."

"Right."

It's not a lie. That is what Odelia does for a living. She just never specified to Dad what kind of counseling it is that she does.

"You know . . ." He turns off the engine and rubs the spot where his beard used to be. "Ramona is a counselor, too."

"I know, Dad." Calla furtively puts her hand on the door handle, not wanting to make it obvious that she's trying to escape the conversation.

"That's pretty coincidental, don't you think? Two counselors, living next door to each other?"

"I don't know . . . not really." She starts to open the door.

"Calla."

Uh-oh.

"Yeah?"

"Your grandmother and Ramona . . . they're not just regular counselors, are they." It isn't a question.

"Ramona told you that?"

"No. I figured it out all by myself." He gives her a tight smile. "And I guess I'm right. They're . . . what do they call themselves?"

"Not 'New-Age freaks.'" She can't help but be relieved—not just that he's smiling at all, but that it's out in the open at last.

"So what are they? Psychic counselors?"

"That pretty much sums it up. How did you figure it out?"

"For one thing, a lot of people around here seem to have signs on their houses advertising themselves as psychic counselors, and the like. I saw the empty bracket at Ramona's, and the bracket with that potted plant here—" He gestures at Odelia's porch, where a tired, straggly looking chrysanthemum

hangs in place of the shingle that reads ODELIA LAUDER, REG-
ISTERED MEDIUM.

"I don't have to be a so-called psychic myself to have figured
out that something is conspicuously missing," Dad tells her.

So-called psychic.

Calla tries not to let the note of skepticism bother her.
After all, she reacted the same way when she first arrived in
the Dale.

"For another thing," Dad goes on, "Ramona likes to talk.
A lot," he adds, but not without affection. "She's the type who
doesn't hold anything back, you know?"

"I know."

"But when it comes to talking about her work . . . well, I
haven't been able to get her to open up about what, exactly,
she does. She always manages to change the subject."

"She doesn't want you to know, Dad. Gammy doesn't,
either."

"Why not?"

"I guess they were worried you wouldn't like it."

"So they were protecting themselves—and you. Is that it?"

"I guess so," she says reluctantly, marveling at the fact that
they're still sitting here talking about this, instead of packing
their bags and making plane reservations.

Dad nods, still rubbing his phantom beard.

He still doesn't know about me.

Should she tell him?

He seems to be taking this pretty well.

Then again—it's one thing for him to know that Odelia
and Ramona are practicing mediums.

It's another for him to find out that his own daughter is dabbling in spiritualism.

"Does it bother you?" he asks, turning to look at Calla at last. "That they do what they do?"

"Why would it?" She shrugs. "I respect it, just like I'd respect any other career."

"I just don't like the idea of anyone taking money from naive strangers who believe in all this stuff."

There are so many things wrong with that statement that Calla doesn't know where to begin.

"Dad, people come to them willingly. Some of them come back over and over again, so they're not strangers. And they're not naive. And it's not like Gammy and Ramona are con artists preying on innocent people. I mean . . . geez, Dad, look around you." She indicates Odelia's modest cottage, and Ramona's next door. "Does it look like they're rolling in dough? Wouldn't they be, if it was all a con game?"

"Good point."

"They help people. That's why they do it. Not for money."

"Okay. I guess it just bothers me that they have you believing in it, too."

"In what?"

"You know . . . hocus-pocus."

"It's not hocus-pocus, Dad. It's nothing like that!"

"Then what do you call it when someone is dabbling in ghosts, and predicting the future, and . . . whatever. Tarot cards? Evil curses?"

"No! Not evil curses. Geez . . . evil curses? It's not like that at all."

"You went to see a psychic. And it got you into trouble. Not just trouble . . . *danger*. You almost *died*, Calla."

"But not because I went to see a psychic."

Or because I am one.

"If you hadn't gone, you wouldn't have come into contact with that horrible woman."

"If I hadn't gone, we wouldn't have known she killed Mom and—"

Oops.

Darrin, she had been about to say.

Thank goodness she caught herself.

"If you hadn't gone," Dad responds, "Sharon Logan wouldn't have tried to kill you."

"But she'd still be on the streets, where she could hurt someone else."

He's silent.

"Dad, you can't blame what happened on what goes on around Lily Dale. The spiritualists here—they help people. Not hurt them. They warned me about the water."

"Who did?"

She hesitates. "A few people here. They said they had visions of me struggling in water. They said to be careful."

"Why weren't you?"

"I was. But . . ." She shrugs. "It's complicated. I guess some things are just meant to happen."

Dad seems to weigh that before saying, "I never believed that anyone can know about them before they happen."

Believed.

As in . . . past tense.

"So you do now?" Calla asks him.

"I don't know what I believe. If it's true that a psychic's vision led you to Geneseo and Sharon Logan—"

"It's true."

"Then how can I argue with reality?"

Calla's hand relaxes on the car door handle at last. "Right," she says softly. "That's how I saw it when I first got here."

"Look, I'm a scientist. I'm always open to new theories. I just wish you had told me from the start what was going on."

"I was afraid you'd make me leave." She hesitates. "You're not going to do that, are you?"

There's a long silence.

Uh-oh.

"I don't know *what* to do about all of this, Calla. But I don't think uprooting you again is a good idea. We shouldn't go back to Tampa—at least not for a long time. Too many bad memories there. And there's no reason to go to California, either, now that I've taken a leave of absence. I suppose there are other places we could visit . . . settle. Uncle Scott and Aunt Susie have offered—"

"No!" Calla says sharply. "Please, Dad."

Her father's only brother asked her to come stay with them in Chicago after Mom died. Calla probably should have been grateful for the offer, and they probably meant well, but she suspects they saw her as a built-in babysitter for her four young cousins.

"They're family," he reminds her.

She knows they are. But they don't feel as much like family as Odelia does. Or even the Taggarts, and the Yorks, and—

"Don't worry," Dad says. "We aren't going to Chicago. Not anytime soon, anyway. You're in school here. You have friends, and . . . I kind of like Lily Dale."

"Really?"

He shrugs. "It's a beautiful place. And I like the change of seasons. And the people are . . . interesting. Friendly. I enjoy them."

"Like Ramona?"

"Sure. Like Ramona." He pauses. "Calla, she and I are . . . well, I'm kind of rusty at this kind of thing, so I'm not sure what you call it these days. Hooking up?"

Calla wrinkles her nose. "Dating?" she suggests.

"They still call it that?"

Calla shrugs. "Nobody really wants to hear their dad going around talking about hooking up."

"Point taken. So anyway, if it bothers you that Ramona and I are . . . dating . . . then . . ."

"Then you'll break up with her?"

He looks vaguely alarmed.

She can't help but laugh. "Relax, Dad. It doesn't bother me, as long as you don't get your heart broken—and as long as she doesn't, either, because I really like Ramona."

"I wish I could make that guarantee, sweetie, but it doesn't work that way. Relationships are tricky."

Calla thinks of Jacy, and of Kevin, and nods.

She sees her father glance up at Ramona's house. The lights are on and there are silhouettes in the living room window.

"Why don't you go over there, Dad? She's probably seen that we're back from dinner."

"She probably has. But I'll stay here with you until Odelia gets back from . . . where is she, again?"

"She's doing a message circle." No longer any reason to mince words.

"A message circle," he repeats. "What is that?"

"It's . . . it's, like, a gathering where a medium brings spirit messages to people."

"Spirit messages. From the dead."

"Right."

"So—let's just say I were to buy into this stuff," he says cautiously, "and I went to a message circle. Then . . . what?"

"Then you might get a message from the Other Side."

"From whom?"

"From the medium."

"No, I mean—the medium delivers the message from . . . ?"

"From anyone. Your great aunt Tillie, or, I don't know, Abraham Lincoln, or . . ."

"Or Mom."

"It doesn't work like that, Dad. It's not like a telephone line to the Other Side, where you can just place a call to someone you want to speak to."

How many people said pretty much the same thing to Calla since she arrived here, desperate to connect with her mother?

Far too many.

But that hasn't stopped the longing.

Yes, there have been a few incidences—like the other night, in her room, when Calla glimpsed a younger version of her mother. . . .

And last week, when she felt a fleeting embrace and knew,

somehow, without a doubt, that it was Mom's spirit there with her.

But that wasn't enough.

She needs . . .

I need to see her one last time, speak to her one last time.

I need to understand her.

I need to know how she could have done what she did.

How she could have let Darrin do what he did.

"Dad," she says abruptly, "you should go over to Ramona's. I'll be fine here on my own."

"I'm not going to leave you alone here when there's no reason for it."

"Sure there is. I stay here alone all the time. And I have homework to do."

"I thought you said you did it before dinner."

Oops. She did say that . . . but it wasn't true.

"I should study my math."

"Math. That's right—I'll help you," he says firmly, opening the car door and swinging out his legs. "You've got to get those grades up. We're going to work until you have a firm grasp on calculus."

"That's going to take all night."

"Not a problem. I happen to have all night."

It's no use protesting, Calla realizes, following her father into the house.

Gert is there, waiting by the front door. Miriam is there, too, sitting quietly in the living room, stitching on an embroidery hoop.

She looks up briefly when Calla and her father enter, then goes back to her needlework.

She's seen a lot, over the years. Family dramas playing themselves out within the walls of her beloved home; various residents coming and going: Aunt Katie and Jack Lauder and . . .

Mom.

Miriam must have known about the baby.

But she probably isn't going to reveal any of the details to Calla.

I have to ask Gammy about it.

And she will. Next chance she gets.

"I was thinking," Dad interrupts her thoughts, "that it would be nice for the two of us to go look at a couple of colleges this weekend."

"Really?"

He nods. "What do you say?"

"Which schools?"

"Penn State. Cornell. Maybe Colgate."

Cornell.

Kevin is there.

When they were in Florida, she overheard him telling Dad that he'd show them around campus if they came to visit.

"I don't know," she says. "Maybe we shouldn't do that this weekend."

That would mean she'd have to miss her Beginning Mediumship class two weeks in a row. She really can't afford to do that. She needs all the tune-in/tune-out help she can get.

"Calla, you have some decisions to make about where you're going next year. By now, your mother would have had you filling out applications for early decision. I really dropped the ball. We've got to go look at some campuses and figure out where you want to go."

"But—"

"We can't put it off any longer. I'm not asking you. I'm telling you. We're taking a road trip this weekend. I'll pick you up at school on Friday and we'll get right on the road. Got it?"

She sighs. "Got it."

She was right about having him here. Her life is no longer her own.

THIRTEEN

Lily Dale
Thursday, October 11
2:10 a.m.

Calla is on an airplane, soaring high above an urban skyline.

"Those of you folks who are seated on the left-hand side of the plane will recognize Lady Liberty there in the harbor," the pilot announces, and Calla leans her head against the window to see.

Lady Liberty.

New York City.

Through the window, she recognizes the familiar patina of the statue, perched on an island the size of a dime.

"And there's the spire of the Empire State Building," the pilot continues, "and the building with the slanted top is Citicorp. . . ."

Calla spots both.

"That over there is Thirty Rockefeller Plaza, where you'll be able to see the Christmas tree and go skating in just a few months."

The plane swoops lower.

High atop 30 Rock, a tiny figure is waving.

"Who is that, Captain?" Calla calls, but there's no reply.

They circle the building, spiraling lower and lower.

Now Calla can see that the figure is female.

She looks young—maybe Calla's age, maybe a little older.

She's wearing an old-fashioned calico dress with an apron and a matching sunbonnet identical to the one Odelia had on in the garden. It shades her face so that Calla can't make out her features, but there's something familiar about her.

"Who is that?" she asks again, but nobody replies.

The plane drops lower still.

I know her. There's something so familiar about her. If only I could see her face. . . .

"Who is she? Can someone please tell me?"

"She's your sister," says the passenger in the next seat.

A passenger whose voice is hauntingly familiar.

Shocked, Calla turns to see her mother sitting there.

"Mom!"

Even as she cries out, her mother vanishes.

She jerks her head toward the window again, but the waving girl has disappeared as well, along with the buildings, and the sky, and . . .

With a gasp, Calla sits up in bed.

It was just a dream.

Of course it was.

She doesn't have a sister.

The baby died.

She sinks back against the pillows, staring into the blackness, her heart still pounding.

It's a long time before she drifts back to sleep.

FOURTEEN

Lily Dale
Thursday, October 11
7:54 a.m.

"So . . . he knows," Calla tells Evangeline as soon as they round the bend in Dale Drive on the way to school beneath a steely gray sky.

There's a pause as Evangeline—who, before Calla interrupted, was wondering aloud what to wear when she and Russell go to the movies together on Friday night—digests this information.

"He does?" she asks, wide-eyed.

The cool thing about Evangeline is that she can shift gears pretty easily.

Another cool thing is that she's tuned in to Calla well

enough to know exactly what she's talking about without having to have it spelled out for her.

"You told him?"

"No. He figured it out."

"Wow. I've been so careful not to say anything, and my aunt has, too."

Calla doesn't bother to tell her Ramona's uncharacteristic silence on the topic of her work might be what tipped off her father.

No need for anyone to feel guilty about the cat being let out of the bag. It was bound to happen sooner or later.

And Calla has realized, in the last twelve hours or so, that sooner is better than later.

Last night, while she and Dad were going over her math problems, she was a lot more comfortable than she has been in a long time. It's easier to spend time with him when there's nothing left to hide.

Well, there are a couple of things. . . .

Like the fact that Calla herself has supernatural abilities.

And the fact that Mom had another child.

But even Evangeline doesn't know about that.

And Calla doesn't want to think about it now. Not with last night's strange dream still lingering, still oddly clear, almost as if . . .

No.

She doesn't have a sister.

Maybe she did once.

But she's dead, along with both her parents.

"Wow . . . how much did your dad figure out?" Evangeline

glances at the sky, then holds out her hand to see if drops are starting to fall.

"Everything. About your aunt and my grandmother being mediums . . . along with pretty much everyone else in town."

"Including you."

"No. Not including me." Calla feels a raindrop land on her hand and flips up the hood on the fleece jacket she pulled on this morning. The temperature must have dropped at least thirty degrees overnight. So much for Indian summer.

"I thought you said he knew everything," Evangeline reminds her, flipping up her own hood.

"Yeah, but not that."

Not about Mom, either. But it's only a matter of time.

"Why didn't you just tell him about yourself?"

"Because I'm afraid to," she says simply. "I mean, he's surprisingly okay with the two of us living here with all of this stuff he doesn't understand going on around us. But I think he'd be a lot less okay if he realized that I'm directly involved."

"I think you're right."

"The other thing is, he's decided he's taking me away this weekend to go looking at colleges—including Cornell."

"Doesn't your ex-boyfriend go there?"

"You got it," she says grimly. "I just saw him in Florida, and he kind of wanted to get back together."

"You told him no?"

"Of course. He broke my heart. No way am I putting it out there again with him, especially now that . . ."

"Now that you have Jacy. It's okay. You can say it."

"It doesn't bother you?"

Evangeline shrugs. "If he had to fall in love with one of us—and it couldn't be me—then I'm glad it's you."

Calla can't help but grin at that, even as she protests, "He's not in love with me."

"Oh, yeah, he is. I saw you guys walking together the other day, and it was totally obvious. I've never seen him look that comfortable ever, anywhere, unless he was running."

"Really?"

"Yeah. But listen, about Cornell—just because your old boyfriend is there doesn't mean you shouldn't go look at it."

"True."

"Or that you shouldn't go there, if you want to. I mean, it's a huge school."

Also true. But . . .

Hearing tires crunching on the road behind them, she turns to see Blue Slayton in his BMW.

"Want a ride?" he calls out the window.

"Definitely!" Evangeline answers for both of them. "It's going to start pouring any second."

Then, with a belated glance at Calla, she asks in a low voice, "You don't mind, right? I left my umbrella at school the other day. Unless you have one?"

"No. It's okay, we can ride with Blue." She hasn't seen much of him since they mutually, and without discussing it, concluded they're better off as friends.

He leans over and opens the passenger-side door. A pair of crutches are propped in the backseat. Evangeline scrambles in beside them, leaving Calla to sit in front with Blue.

"How's your leg?" she asks, thinking she probably should have called to ask him about it when she got back to town.

He was injured a few weeks ago in a soccer game, the night before she was supposed to go to the homecoming dance with him.

"It's better. How was your trip to Florida?"

"Great," she lies, not wanting to get into it.

"What'd you do?"

"Oh, you know . . . the usual Florida stuff."

"The weather was great, right?"

Was it? That was so far off her radar, given what happened, that there could have been a hurricane and she probably wouldn't remember.

"Sure," she agrees, because it's easier that way. "The weather was great, and I hung out with my old friends."

"Yeah. I kept seeing you there."

Seeing her?

Oh! He means in a psychic vision, of course.

"What did you see?" she asks cautiously, aware that now he's going to ask her about Sharon Logan, and about her mother, and maybe even about the baby.

And then she's going to have to explain it all to Evangeline, too.

Life was so much less complicated when she wasn't surrounded by people who know as much—or more—about what she's been doing than she does.

"You know, you were in the water—couldn't tell if it was a pool or the Gulf," Blue says.

Now he's going to tell me someone was trying to drown me, and he's going to ask why . . . unless he already knows.

"You were wearing a bathing suit, and you looked great in it, of course—and you were really relaxed, and there were palm trees, you know, and a bunch of people. You were having a great time."

"Really?" Calla doesn't dare look at Evangeline, who now knows the truth about what happened there.

Calla hasn't worn a bathing suit in ages.

And her time in the water was hardly relaxing.

"Yeah, really." Blue flashes her his familiar, flirty smile. "I like to keep tabs on you, you know?"

Uneasy, she watches the wipers' rhythmic arc across the rain-spattered windshield. "Well, anyway . . . thanks for picking us up. I thought your dad didn't like you to drive to school."

That's because Blue got a speeding ticket one morning, doing sixty in a school zone.

"Yeah, well, he doesn't have much choice. I mean, what am I supposed to do? Hobble down the road on crutches?"

"He could drop you off," Evangeline points out.

"Yeah, he *could* . . . if he were around. But he's not."

Typical. Blue's father, David Slayton, is a celebrity medium who spends far more time in front of television cameras in New York and LA than he does with his son in Lily Dale.

Calla has only met the man once, and was unnerved by his warning that she was going to find herself in a dangerous situation. He didn't specify water, as others had, but somehow, his warning left just as great an impact on her.

But . . . what about Blue?

Why is he talking about things that didn't happen, as if he's trying hard—too hard—to convince her of his psychic abilities?

Maybe because he doesn't have any, she realizes, and her stomach turns a little.

Maybe, living in his father's larger-than-life shadow, Blue

feels obligated to live up to a larger-than-life reputation. And maybe he thinks that the only way he can do that is to lie.

Sitting beside him, driving toward the school, Calla is certain she made the right choice when she chose Jacy over Blue, the guy all the Lily Dale High girls want.

With Jacy, what you see is what you get.

He doesn't play games, and he doesn't pretend to be someone he's not.

They pull into the crowded school parking lot, and Blue instantly finds an empty spot close to the door.

"This is a miracle," Evangeline declares, as he turns off the engine. "I thought you'd have to park in, like, the next state. How'd you manage this?"

"Guess I was born under a lucky star. Hey, Calla, can I talk to you for a second?"

Uh-oh.

"Sure."

As Evangeline scrambles out of the backseat, she raises her brows at Calla, who shrugs.

She has no idea what Blue wants to talk about, but she has a feeling it's not the weather.

"See you later, guys. Thanks for the ride, Blue."

"No problem."

Evangeline closes the door behind her, leaving them alone in the car to watch her splash off through the rain toward the redbrick school.

"Calla . . ."

She turns toward him reluctantly, wondering what to say if he asks her out again. She can tell him she can't because of Jacy, though she and Jacy haven't exactly discussed whether they're free to see other people. She knows she doesn't want to, and she's pretty sure he doesn't either.

"What's up, Blue?" she asks breezily, as if she's expecting him to ask her what the cafeteria is serving for lunch today.

"Before my dad left for London last night, he asked me if I'd seen you lately. I kind of . . . told him you were away."

Puzzled, she says, "That's okay. I was."

"No, I mean . . . I told him you were *still* away last night. And that I didn't know when you were coming back."

"You lied? Why?"

"Because I didn't want him bugging you."

"Bugging me?" she echoes. "Why would he bug me?"

"He can be really pushy. I wasn't even going to tell you about this, but . . . well, he called again this morning to ask if you were back yet. He hardly ever calls when he's on the road, especially from overseas. I told him you were coming back today and that I'd let you know he wants to talk to you."

"What about, though?"

"Something that I'm sure is none of his business," Blue says with a scowl.

"What is it?"

"I'm not sure, exactly. He wouldn't tell me. All he said was that it's about your mother."

"Tell me, Calla, how is everything going?" asks Mrs. Erskine, an attractive thirty-something blonde who has a framed, recent wedding photo on her desk.

How is everything going? You mean other than the fact that my mother's dead, my father's here, someone tried to kill me over the weekend, and I have no idea what I want to do next year?

"Everything's going great!" She smiles so brightly her face hurts.

"I'm glad." Mrs. Erskine opens a manila folder. "Your transcript shows that you were a straight-A student back in Florida. And your grades are very good so far this term . . . other than math, I see."

She waits for Calla to reply.

What am I supposed to say to that?

"I'm kind of having a hard time getting used to how it, um, works here."

As if math works differently in this part of the country.

Yeah, right.

Mrs. Erskine sort of nods, and Calla can tell she's thinking that's no excuse. A formula is a formula.

She looks away, at the rain-spattered windowpane and the gray world beyond.

"I can recommend some tutors so that you can—"

"Oh, I don't need a tutor. Willow York is my study partner, and my dad is helping me, too."

"Your father?" Mrs. Erskine glances quickly at the folder, then up again. "But he's in California, and it might be more helpful for you to work with someone who's—"

"No," Calla interrupts again, "actually, he's here now."

"For a visit?"

"To stay." She pauses. "For a while." She pauses again, conscious of the woman's intent stare. "Or maybe for good."

"I'm glad. It's a good idea for you two not to be separated after . . . all you've been through."

Mrs. Erskine doesn't know the half of it.

Uncomfortable, Calla looks at her watch. "Um . . . you had said you wanted to see me about college applications?"

"Yes, and there's no time to waste. Did you make your list for me?"

Calla is already digging in her backpack for the sheet of notebook paper she hastily filled out last night before bed.

She hands it across the guidance counselor's desk and watches as she scans the list, nodding. "Penn State, Colgate, Cornell . . ."

"Those are my reach schools," Calla says hastily. "My father is going to take me to see the campuses this weekend."

"All great places." Mrs. Erskine gives her an approving smile.

Yes, they are. But they're only on Calla's list because her father mentioned visiting them.

"Northwestern," Mrs. Erskine continues, and Calla nods.

The counselor seems to be waiting for her to say something about it.

"My father's family lives in Chicago," she says. "He grew up there, so he thought . . . you know, that I might want to go to school there."

"*Do* you?"

"Um . . ."

Mrs. Erskine lowers the list and looks at her. "Calla, you're the one who should make the decision about where you want to go. Don't apply to schools that don't interest you. Really. It's a waste of everybody's time."

"I guess you can cross off Northwestern, then."

It's not as if Dad will mind. He was merely making suggestions. She wrote down most of them for lack of anything better.

"How about Florida? You've listed a few schools there."

"I know. It's where I'm from, so I thought . . ." Again, she hesitates.

In truth, Lisa urged Calla to apply to the same schools on her list. She wants to be roommates, maybe even sorority sisters. It's what they had always planned on, from the time they were little girls.

But a lot has changed since then.

"Do you want to go back to Florida, Calla?" Mrs. Erskine asks.

"I'm not sure. Not really."

"Where do you want to go?"

To her horror, she feels hot tears spring to her eyes, and looks down quickly to hide them. "I don't know. I guess I don't really want to go anywhere."

"You don't want to go to college?"

"No, I do, but . . ." She takes a deep breath and forces herself to look up, trying not to blink and release the tears. "It's coming up so soon, and . . . I like it here. That's why I stayed for the school year. I never got to spend time with my grandmother, and I've never been to Lily Dale until a few months ago. It's where my mother grew up. I guess now that I'm here, I don't really want to leave."

She sees a flash of understanding—and sympathy—in Mrs. Erskine's blue eyes. "That makes sense."

"But I feel like such a baby—like I'm afraid to leave home."

"Calla . . ." The counselor reaches across the desk and touches her hand. "You've already left home. Under circumstances much more difficult than most kids your age will face in a lifetime. You're not a baby. You're one of the bravest young women I've ever known."

She's never thought of it that way.

Now the tears are rolling down her cheeks, and Mrs. Erskine hands her a tissue.

"Look, maybe you should just focus on local schools. If you want to transfer down the road, you can, but . . ." She reaches over and opens a desk drawer. "I'm going to give you some information on Fredonia State University. Ever heard of it?"

Calla nods. Her mother went there, for undergrad. She told Calla that she was desperate to go away but couldn't afford to.

"It's just a few miles down the road, and it's an excellent school." Mrs. Erskine rummages through her drawer, plucking things from folders. "There are a few other good schools in Buffalo—not all that far away, either."

"Thank you." Calla gratefully accepts the packets the counselor hands her.

"Look them over, and talk to your father. I think you should go see the schools he wants to show you this weekend, too. You never know—you might fall in love with one of them."

Yeah, that, or fall in love—all over again—with my old boyfriend who goes to one of them, Calla thinks grimly.

Cornell is out of the question for her. With Kevin there, she'd only be asking for trouble.

That reminds her. She never did check her e-mail. Lisa said he sent her one. She probably has a bunch of others, too.

Later tonight, she decides, she'll pull out the laptop again. Just to take care of her own business.

Not to stick her nose further into her mother's.

FIFTEEN

New York City
Thursday, October 11
8:41 a.m.

According to Liz Jessee—the world's friendliest landlady—Hell's Kitchen, in the heart of Manhattan's West Side, was once a desolate stretch of the city.

Now, Hell's Kitchen—and thus, Liz Jessee's no-frills five-story brick building—is in a desirable location, entirely convenient to restaurants, theaters, and midtown office buildings.

Laura is headed toward one of them right now, having just received a new short-term assignment from her temp agency.

As she descends the last flight of steps from her top floor studio apartment, she consults the address she scribbled on a scrap of paper when the assignment came in twenty minutes ago.

She's been in New York long enough to know that she'll have to head uptown, and east, to get there.

She'll walk, of course. She doesn't take the subway unless an assignment takes her all the way down to the financial district. Not just because Laura finds the subway unnerving, but because she can't afford it. She still has three more days until payday, and she'll be lucky if she can scrape together enough money to eat.

When Geraldine, her supervisor at the temp agency, told her that today's assignment was at a company called Overseas Corporate Funds, she expected it to be downtown near Wall Street, too. Midtown was a pleasant surprise.

She arranges her shoulder bag in a cross-chest, mugger-proof position and steps outside to find Liz Jessee sweeping the stoop.

A pleasant woman in her midsixties, she looks up with a smile. "Good morning, Laura."

"Hi, Liz."

"It feels like July out here, doesn't it?"

Laura realizes that the sun is already beaming warmly from a clear blue sky and wonders whether she should have worn her other suit. She only has two, and she wore the other one yesterday. But this one is wool.

"So it's going to be hot again today?" she asks Liz, who has a way of knowing these things. She's plugged into the weather, the news, even the neighborhood gossip.

"Near ninety. Of course, where I grew up, that's nothing."

"Where did you grow up?"

"Florida."

Florida.

An image flashes into Laura's head: palm trees, the ocean . . . and, standing in the sand, an attractive, brown-haired woman wearing a charcoal gray business suit with shiny black buttons, carrying a briefcase.

It's such an odd image.

Why did it pop into Laura's head?

Things do, sometimes. Things that don't make sense.

And, once in a while, things that do make sense, but only later. When something—or someone—she's imagined in her head or seen in a dream shows up in real life.

When she was really little, she used to find herself inexplicably thinking about a stained-glass window filled with interlocking loops of rose-and-green-colored glass. The window had a distinctive shape: rectangular on the bottom half and curving up to a point on the top half.

It popped into Laura's head pretty often—particularly when her mother was cruel to her. Somehow, it made her feel better. She even used to draw pictures of it, with crayons.

It wasn't until she was older that she actually came across it. She was returning from running an errand for Mother—taking the long way back to Center Street to delay having to go home—that she saw that window on the rectory door tucked away beside a church.

The coincidence was so startling that she found herself drawn from the sidewalk to the door, mesmerized.

Then the door opened, and a man dressed in black with a white collar stood smiling down at her.

"Down south, it wasn't considered hot unless the thermometer broke a hundred," Liz chatters on. You're not used to this kind of heat, though, are you, Laura? Coming from Minnesota."

For the hundredth time, Laura regrets the lie she told Liz Jessee when she moved in.

Why Minnesota?

Why not someplace she's actually been?

Because you haven't been anywhere that wasn't too close to Geneseo for comfort, she reminds herself.

Anyway, she knows enough about Minnesota to realize the temperature doesn't break a hundred degrees there on a regular basis.

"Back home," she tells Liz, for good measure, "it isn't considered cold unless the thermometer drops below zero."

"Is that right. Well, it's supposed to turn colder tonight— a front coming in from the west—but nowhere near zero. I'll bet you'll be homesick for that kind of weather when December rolls around, because we don't get much snow around here. Unless you're going to be going back home for the holidays?"

"I . . . I'm not sure."

"Well, if you don't, you'll have to join Jim and me for Christmas dinner. We have a whole big crowd."

"I couldn't intrude on your family celebration."

"Oh, it's not family, other than us and our daughter. Every year, I invite people who have nowhere else to go."

That pretty much describes me, Laura thinks. It describes her even before she landed in New York, alone.

"This year, we'll have a couple of the other new neighbors, and some of Jim's coworkers, and José who runs the bodega two blocks down on Ninth."

Laura buys her *New York Post* at that bodega, when she can spare a couple of quarters. José must be the silent, smiling man who is always behind the counter. "Is he a friend of yours?"

"Sure. I mean, we don't get together for lunch, or anything, but I consider him a friend. I love meeting new people. Someone once told me I could talk to a wall," Liz confides cheerfully. "One of my favorite things to do is people-watch. You know—see a stranger and try to guess what his life is like by the way he dresses or talks, or by his body language. Know what I mean?"

"Yes."

And people who like to people-watch make me nervous.

All she wants is to live an anonymous life, and she came to the largest city on the East Coast hoping it would be possible.

She can't find you now, though.

She's in jail.

Unless . . .

What if, by some fluke, she's out?

What if she follows the trail Laura tried so hard to cover and finds her way to New York City?

If she finds her way here, to this Hell's Kitchen address, and asks Liz about Laura, Liz—who can talk to a wall—is bound to spill the details.

I can always ask her not to, if anyone comes looking for me.

But that might make her suspicious.

She might go to the police.

Then what?

Laura glances at her watch and tries to sound casual as she tells Liz, "I have to get going. I've got a new temp job and I've never been to this address before."

"Oh, where is it? Maybe I can give you directions."

"I'm pretty sure I know where I'm going."

"But you don't want to get lost," Liz persists. "What's the address?"

Laura consults the scrap of paper in her hand. "It's Thirty Rockefeller Plaza."

SIXTEEN

Lily Dale
Thursday, October 11
3:31 p.m.

"Wow, you're moving in slow motion today," Evangeline comments as she and Calla head toward home after school beneath a shared umbrella. "Are you feeling okay?"

"It's not that, it's just . . ." Calla hesitates, idly watching a pair of spirit orbs floating past them.

This morning, she had been planning to tell Evangeline on the way to school about the detectives. But then they started talking about Jacy, and about Cornell, and then Blue gave them a ride, and she didn't get the chance.

Now that the meeting is imminent, she's not sure she's in the mood to discuss it.

Then again, Evangeline knows something is wrong.

And sometimes, she reminds herself, it helps to talk about things. Lately, her tendency has been to keep things bottled up until her emotions explode every which way. That's not good for anyone.

And the Lily Dale gate is visible just ahead. Time is running out.

"So, remember how I told you that I had to talk to the police back in Florida about what happened?"

"Yeah?"

"Well, they're here now, and they want to talk to me again. And I'm kind of scared."

"About what they're going to tell you?"

"About that," she takes a deep breath, "and about what I'm going to tell them."

Quickly, she fills in the details Evangeline didn't already know about the baby, about Darrin's murder and the connection to her mother's.

"Wow, Calla." Evangeline drapes a supportive arm around her shoulders. "Do you want me to come with you to talk to the detectives?"

"No, I know you have your Crystal Healing class in a little while."

"I can skip it."

"No, you should go. I'll be okay. My grandmother will be there."

"What about your dad?"

Calla shakes her head. "He doesn't know."

"Don't you think he should?"

"Yes, but I don't want him to hear every last detail. At least, not from me. If he's there, I know I won't be able to talk."

"I don't think I would, either. Wow, Calla. Poor you."

Yeah. Poor me, she thinks.

But she forces a smile at Evangeline. "I'll get through it. Things can only get better, right?"

"Definitely."

They've reached the gate, which is untended at this time of year. As they pass the gatehouse, Calla is surprised to see a man sitting there. Then she realizes he's wearing Victorian clothing, and isn't exactly solid.

He tips his hat at her with a smile, and she can't help but smile back.

"Hey, what did Blue want to talk to you about this morning?" Evangline asks. "Wait—don't tell me. He wants to go out with you again, right?"

"Wrong."

"Really? Because I figured that the second he saw you with Jacy, he'd want you back."

"He never had me," Calla points out.

"Yeah, funny how he didn't realize that, don't you think?"

She doesn't know what to think about Blue, and right now, he's not the Slayton she's worried about.

"Evangeline, he said his father wants to talk to me about my mother."

"Whoa."

"I know."

"That's pretty amazing. When it comes to David Slayton, there's no fooling around. He totally means business. Unlike his son."

"What do you mean?"

"I mean, Blue Slayton is a big fat fraud. I've been hearing

people say that for years, but I figured they were just jealous. Nope. He's about as psychic as that rock."

She gestures at a large boulder on the side of the road. As she looks at it, Calla sees a familiar impish figure materialize on top of it: the little Depression-era kid she's seen a few times now.

He balances on one foot, pretends to lose his balance, then turns and grins at Calla, clearly taunting her.

Half amused, half irritated, she turns away.

"You don't know for sure that Blue isn't psychic," she points out to Evangeline.

"Come on, I just pointed out that if he were so psychic, he would have figured out that he didn't have you wrapped around his finger like all the other girls, and maybe he would have figured out that you were into Jacy, too. But he didn't, did he? Did he ever even ask you about it?"

"No," Calla admits.

"And did you hear the stuff he said about your Florida trip? I mean, you weren't exactly lounging around on the beach in a bathing suit, were you?"

"No, but—"

"If Blue had any intuition, he would have sensed that you weren't okay. I mean, it's not like I'm the best medium in town—or anywhere close—but even *I* had a feeling something was wrong last weekend."

"I know."

"So why didn't he?" Evangeline doesn't wait for a response. "I'll tell you why not. Because he fakes his abilities."

"I never heard him say he was a medium," Calla points out. "It's not like he's got a shingle hanging with his name on it."

"No, but people are always saying he's, like, the son of this supergifted medium."

"I thought people are always saying he's a fraud."

Evangeline shrugs. "Different people say different things. You've hung out with him. What do *you* think?"

"I think it must be really hard to be Blue Slayton."

And she's got to get in touch with David Slayton as soon as possible.

Blue gave her his cell phone number but warned her that he doesn't like to keep it turned on when he's traveling and doing readings. He says it interferes with spirit energy.

"Well, does he check his messages?" she asked, wondering how Blue feels about not being able to reach his father if he needs him.

"Usually. But not every day."

Great. David Slayton is in England through the weekend, conducting a series of psychic seminars. If he doesn't get her message before she leaves with Dad on Friday after school, she'll have no choice but to wait until Monday and wonder what he can possibly have to tell her about Mom.

There's an unfamiliar dark sedan parked at the curb when Calla reaches her grandmother's house.

"They're here," Evangeline observes. "Are you sure you don't want me to come in with you?"

No. She isn't sure at all.

But Evangeline has her class to go to, and anyway, Odelia's car is here, too. She'll lend moral support if Calla needs it.

Who is she kidding?

She'll definitely need it.

"I'll be okay," she tells Evangeline.

"Call me later and let me know how it goes."

"I will."

"And tell them everything, Calla. They need to know."

"I will," she promises again, and steps out from beneath Evangeline's umbrella.

Looking up at the house, she's reluctant to go in. But it's raining, and she can't linger out here another second without showing up drenched.

She makes a dash for the porch, hearing Evangeline call, "Good luck!" after her.

Opening the front door, she prepares herself for the grim mood that will undoubtedly greet her on the other side.

Instead, she hears raucous laughter as she steps into the front hall.

That must mean she was wrong about the car out front; the detectives aren't here yet. Maybe a friend stopped by to visit Gammy. Or a walk-in client with a great sense of humor.

"That was a good one, Odelia!" a male voice is saying, and another male voice emits the kind of sigh one emits after laughing really, really hard.

Okay, two walk-in clients with great senses of humor. Both men.

Frowning, Calla pokes her head into the living room.

The first person she spots is Odelia.

Then rotund, balding, mustachioed Detective Lutz.

And finally, lanky Detective Kearney, whose Irish green eyes are dancing merrily as Calla's grandmother launches into another joke.

"How about this one? A man walks into a salami shop with a parrot on his—"

Calla clears her throat loudly.

Gammy stops talking abruptly and all three of them look over at her.

"Hello, young lady." Detective Lutz hastily gets to his feet.

"Hello," Calla returns politely, then asks her grandmother, "A salami shop?"

"Never mind. Calla, you remember Detective Lutz and Detective Kearney, right?"

"Yes." She shakes both their hands, hoping they don't notice how clammy her own is.

"How have you been doing since you got back?" Detective Kearney asks. With his blond crewcut and his good-natured smile, he reminds her of someone's big brother.

"I've been great, thanks. How have *you* been?"

He chuckles. "Just fine. And your grandmother is quite the comedian."

"Oh, I don't know about that." Odelia shakes her head modestly.

"We spoke to your father earlier today," Detective Lutz announces, obviously wanting to get things under way.

"You did?" Calla looks at her grandmother in surprise. "I didn't know that."

Odelia nods. "Your dad wanted to be here now, but I told him you might feel more comfortable without him here."

Uh-oh. "What did he say?"

"He said that was fine, and actually, the detectives told him they would prefer to speak to you privately."

"What about you, Gammy? Can you stay?"

She looks at the detectives.

Uh-oh again.

"It's better if we speak to you alone," Kearney says. "Don't worry. We won't bite."

"I'll just be upstairs if you need me," Odelia says, and disappears after planting a kiss on the top of Calla's head.

"We just want to ask you a few more questions, if you don't mind having a seat," Detective Lutz tells her, not unkindly, but with the same no-nonsense demeanor she found intimidating back in Tampa.

He moves from the chair he was sitting in to another that's closer to the couch, saying, "We've been speaking to your friends Patsy and Bob."

"They're not really my, um, friends," she corrects him. "More like . . . you know . . ."

"Acquaintances?" Kearney supplies, and she flashes him a grateful look, nodding.

"They were both very sorry to hear about what happened to you."

They know too, now?

Well, of course they do. How else were the detectives supposed to question them?

Calla figures it's only a matter of time before the news reaches the high school gossip mill. People are going to be asking questions she might not feel comfortable answering.

So what else is new?

"Did Sharon Logan confess to killing my mother?" she asks, hoping the answer is yes. Who knows? Maybe she's already told them what happened to Darrin, too. Then Calla won't have to—

"No," Kearney tells her, "she hasn't said anything."

"Nothing at all?"

"Not a word. No one can get anything out of her. She's basically checked out."

"Wow. That stinks."

The detectives look at each other.

"What if she never talks?" Calla asks. "Do you have enough proof of what she did so that you can keep her in jail?"

"We're working on it. Don't worry." That's Kearney, of course.

Don't worry?

What if that woman gets out of jail and comes after her again?

Noting the look on Detective Kearney's face, Calla realizes he's thinking the same thing. So much for big-brotherly reassurance.

"So, Calla—Lily Dale is quite an interesting place," Detective Lutz says, as if that's news to her.

"Yes, it is," she agrees, not sure what else to say.

"I've never personally worked with a police psychic before, but a lot of detectives do."

Kearney nods vigorously—so vigorously that Calla wonders if he's worked with police psychics himself.

"Are you using a police psychic?" she asks. "You know, on this case?"

"Oh, no. No." Lutz's chins waggle as he shakes his head. "I just want you to know that we're taking very seriously what your friends—your acquaintances—told us."

"Did they tell you something new about Sharon Logan?"

"Not exactly. But there does seem to be some kind of

consensus that she might have committed another serious crime before she came after you."

"You mean, that she killed my mother? Because—"

"No, before that," Kearney tells her. "Both Patsy and Bob mentioned—independent of each other—that they sensed another death around Sharon Logan."

"I know whose it was."

The detectives look at Calla in surprise.

She pulls the folded death notice from her backpack.

"His name," she says flatly, "was Darrin Yates."

SEVENTEEN

New York City
Thursday, October 11
4:59 p.m.

Sitting behind the receptionist's desk, bare except for a message pad, a pen, and a gigantic vase filled with waxy white calla lilies, Laura answers the incessantly ringing telephone again.

"Good afternoon, Overseas Corporate Funds, where may I direct your call?"

"Extension one-five-two, please."

She transfers the call and glances at the clock as she presses the next line. "Good afternoon, Overseas Corporate Funds, where may I direct your call?"

Less than a minute to go.

"Extension one-eighteen."

Transfer. Next line.

"Good afternoon, Overseas Corporate Funds, where may I direct your call?"

No reply.

"Good afternoon?"

Nothing.

Her hand stiffens on the receiver. "Hello?"

There's a click, and then a dial tone.

Laura's heart pounds erratically . . . and for no good reason, she tells herself. When you're a receptionist whose job it is to answer the phone hundreds of times a day, a percentage of those calls are going to be wrong numbers, cranks, hang-ups, whatever.

It doesn't mean anything.

Still . . .

She'll ask the temp agency not to send her back here tomorrow. Just in case.

She looks at the clock again.

It's five.

I'm out of here.

She sets the phone system to go into automated answering, pushes back the rolling chair, gathers her things, and goes to find the office supervisor, Ellen.

"Leaving already?" she asks when Laura hands her the agency's time sheet for a signature.

"It's five o'clock. Those were the hours, right? Nine to five?"

The woman merely gives her wristwatch a pointed glance before scribbling on the time sheet and handing it back to Laura.

"Thank you. Have a good night." She makes a beeline for the elevator.

Funny how all the companies she's worked for over the past few months have stressed the importance of a punctual arrival for their office temps but apparently don't expect the temps to make a punctual departure.

Ordinarily, Laura might have offered to stay later if they needed her.

But not tonight.

Not here.

Not after that strange phone call.

Not so strange at all. You're being paranoid.

It was just a hang-up.

Nobody knows where you are. Least of all, her.

And even if she's somehow found out . . . she's in jail. There's nothing she can do about it.

You're safe here, Laura reassures herself as she steps out onto West Fiftieth Street and is gladly swallowed up by the rush hour pedestrian crowd.

EIGHTEEN

Lily Dale
Thursday, October 11
6:22 p.m.

"You know, Odelia, when you said you were making something special for dinner tonight, I really wasn't sure what to expect." Dad sets down his fork and pushes his empty plate away. "But this was good."

"I'm glad you thought so. Did you like it, Calla?"

"Um . . . sure. Most people wouldn't think to mix ham, cheese, bananas, and potato chips in a casserole," she says, hoping to deflect their attention from the fact that she's barely touched her food once again.

"Oh, I can't take the credit," Odelia says, absently toying with her paper napkin. She, too, has barely touched her food, Calla notices.

She's been pretty quiet all night. Much more so than usual.

"What do you mean you can't take the credit?" Dad asks. "This isn't takeout, is it?"

"No, but I didn't make up the recipe. I saw it on the Food Network."

"Well, I'm sure most people who saw it on the Food Network wouldn't dare give it a try," Dad says, "so you still get a big thumbs-up from me."

"Who am I to argue with that kind of reasoning?"

Odelia starts to get up, but Dad stops her. "I'll get the dishes. You just relax and get your poker face on. Ramona said she'll be over at eight with the cards and a couple of rolls of pennies. The stakes are higher tonight."

"That sounds fun, Jeff, but I can't. I have an appointment coming here."

"This late?"

"Oh, I do appointments at all hours. I'll be done by eight, but . . . maybe you and Ramona can play cards next door?"

"I don't know. I spend so much time over there as it is, I thought a change of scenery would be good."

Calla looks from her father to her grandmother to her father again, wondering what he's up to.

Obviously, he hasn't yet mentioned to Odelia that he's figured out the truth about her. Calla hasn't, either.

Maybe she should have, but she's had much too much on her mind—particularly after the meeting with the detectives.

She told them the whole story.

When they left, she recapped it for Odelia.

Well, most of it.

171

She didn't mention the baby. She was about to, but Dad showed up for dinner.

He asked about her meeting with the detectives, and she could tell her grandmother wanted her to give him the details, but she just couldn't. Not yet.

Not while she was still feeling guilty for telling the police about her mother and Darrin's secret baby.

She felt guilty bringing it up but told herself that it had happened a long time ago. Plus, what if there's some connection between that and what Sharon Logan did to Mom and Darrin?

Is there?

A little voice inside her head—maybe not her own—has been asking that question ever since the detectives left, promising they'd be in touch again soon.

"Odelia, there's something you should know. . . ."

Uh-oh. Calla's attention jerks back to her father.

"What is it, Jeff?"

"I know what kinds of appointments you do."

Odelia pauses before asking, "What kind?"

"I know you're a psychic medium."

Calla has never seen her grandmother's dyed-red eyebrows shoot quite that close to her dyed-red hairline.

"So is Ramona," Dad adds, and leans back in his chair to wait for the reaction.

It takes a moment to get one.

"Ramona didn't tell me she told you."

"She didn't."

Odelia looks at Calla.

"I didn't tell him, Gammy. He figured it out."

"Really." She throws up her hands. "Well, Jeff, you can't blame me for not wanting to tell you. I know how Stephanie always felt about what I do, and I knew she didn't want you or Calla to know."

"Obviously not."

"Are you . . . okay with this?"

"I guess so. As long as I don't have to—you know—witness it, or participate in anything like . . ."

"Like levitating?" Gammy asks, deadpan. "Spoon bending?"

Dad laughs. "Exactly."

What he doesn't know is that she isn't kidding. During the summer season, there are workshops in Lily Dale on both those topics—and more.

No need for baptism by fire, though. Calla figures—or at least, she hopes—that by the time summer rolls around, her father will be as used to life in the Dale as she is.

"So Ramona knows that you know, Jeff?"

He shakes his head.

"Well, you might want to tell her so that she can hang her shingle again. Business is slow at this time of year as it is, and she's losing walk-in traffic."

Dad raises an eyebrow. "Walk-in traffic?"

"Right."

"So . . . what does that mean? People just come here and wander around looking for someone to . . ."

"Do a reading," Calla supplies. "That's how it works."

"But the official season is July and August," Odelia amends, "so you won't see crowds of visitors in the streets at this time of year, and there are no daily programs in the auditorium. In fact, most of the mediums live somewhere else the rest of the year."

"Is that so." Dad looks intrigued, absorbing the information with a lot less animosity than Calla ever imagined. "And it was like this when Stephanie lived here?"

"It's been like this since the town was established as the birthplace of modern spiritualism back in the 1880s."

"I just can't believe she never told me," Dad murmurs, shaking his head.

"She always kept herself separate from what went on around here, Jeff. She was a lot like her father. She even looked just like him."

"That means I must look like him, too," Calla speaks up. It's not the first time she's thought about that—but it's the first time she's dared to bring up the subject of her grandfather since Odelia told her about him the other day.

"Of course you do," her grandmother says agreeably. "You look just like your mother."

Calla dares to voice the question that has been in the back of her mind since their conversation. "Does he know, Gammy? About Mom?"

Odelia hesitates. "I didn't tell him . . . if that's what you're asking."

Dad's eyes widen. "Are you talking about Jack? You're in contact with Jack?"

"No," Odelia says quickly. "I'm not in contact with him. But I know where he is."

"Stephanie didn't."

"Yes, she did. I told her. Years ago."

"But she said—" Dad shakes his head. "She said a lot of

things. And I'm starting to realize that there are a lot of things she didn't say—and could have."

"Some of them might have just been too painful for her." Gammy lays a hand on Dad's arm. "She didn't want anything to do with her father. He hadn't been a part of her life from the time she was a young child—probably too young to remember him."

"I always told her she should try to find him, though. Family is family."

"Yes, and blood is thicker than water. But that didn't stop my daughter from shutting me out of her life, either."

Calla is taken aback by her tone. She's never heard her grandmother speak angrily of Mom.

Now might be a good time to ask Gammy whether they'd had some kind of argument that had driven them apart. Something about dredging the lake.

But . . .

Not with Dad here.

"You know how stubborn Stephanie could be." Dad pats Odelia's arm. "I'm sure she had her regrets. For the record, I encouraged her to mend the fences with you, too."

"I'm sure you did."

"I still can't believe she knew where her father was all along. Why didn't she tell me?"

"Maybe she was afraid you'd talk her into getting in touch with him. And that it would dredge up all those emotions she'd managed to bottle up for years. And that he'd reject her all over again."

"Maybe he wouldn't have," Dad tells her, as Calla wonders if her grandmother is just talking about Mom.

"Well, we'll never know, will we?"

"I don't think it's fair." Calla speaks up at last.

Both Dad and Gammy look at her.

"He should know what happened to Mom. You should have told him, Gammy."

Odelia hesitates. "Maybe I should have, but . . ."

"Why didn't you?"

"Maybe I'm afraid of the same thing Stephanie was."

Dredging up old emotions.

Being rejected all over again.

She never stopped loving him, Calla realizes in surprise, watching her grandmother reach up to brush a tear from the corner of her eye.

And over her shoulder, a pair of figures materialize. One is a striking auburn-haired woman with a coiled bouffant. She has on plaid Bermuda shorts, knee socks, and loafers. She's laughing up at a handsome man with sideburns, wearing a paisley-patterned shirt tucked into peg-leg pants.

They're gone the instant before Calla realizes who they are.

Gammy and her husband, in happier times.

Stunned, she looks across the table and sees, in Odelia's weathered face, a hint of the young beauty she once was.

Her grandmother pushes back her chair abruptly, gets up from the table, and heads for the doorway.

"Where are you going?" Calla asks worriedly, wondering if she, too, caught a glimpse of the past—and couldn't bear it.

"Wait here. I'll be right back."

Odelia disappears into the front of the house.

Calla and her father exchange a glance.

"I probably shouldn't have brought it up," Calla says

guiltily. "You know—about her telling Mom's father that she's . . . gone."

Even now, months later, it's hard for her to say it aloud any other way. *Dead . . . murdered. . . .* Those words are much too harsh.

"No, you were right to say it," Dad assures her. "He deserves to know. He's still her father, no matter what. If it were me . . ."

He falls silent as Odelia returns to the room, carrying a piece of paper.

She hands it to Dad.

"What is it?" Calla asks, leaning over his shoulder.

She sees the name Jack Lauder and a Pennsylvania address in Odelia's spidery handwriting.

"I don't have a phone number. He's unlisted. But that's where he is. Or at least, he was, last I knew."

"Odelia—"

"Calla's right. He deserves to know about Stephanie. And that he has a beautiful granddaughter."

Calla looks questioningly at her father. He folds the slip of paper into his wallet.

"Thank you, Odelia."

She nods.

Seeing the faraway look—and hint of tears—in her grandmother's eyes, Calla knows she's thinking of the wife and mother she once was, and the husband she loved so very long ago.

NINETEEN

Lily Dale
Thursday, October 11
10:26 p.m.

No wonder nobody uses a dial-up connection anymore. It takes forever to accomplish even the simplest online task.

Waiting for her e-mail to load, Calla can hear the faint sound of Ramona's laughter coming from downstairs.

They're still playing poker at the kitchen table. At least, they were, when Calla interrupted her homework an hour ago to go down for a snack. Her appetite had finally drifted back to her as she worked on her math.

Or maybe it was more like, math was so horrible she needed a diversion.

"Come play with us, Calla," Ramona invited, sitting at

the table with Dad, Odelia, and Odelia's friend Andy, who liked to drop in to check on Gert, a product of his cat's recent litter.

"I wish I could, but I have a ton of homework."

Ramona shook her head. "So does Evangeline."

Calla nodded. She had spoken to Evangeline earlier, to fill her in about the meeting with the detectives. When she ended the conversation with a "See you tomorrow morning," Evangeline told her she had to be at school an hour early for extra help in chemistry.

"I keep telling her that working on her homework with Russell isn't a good idea," Ramona said as Andy shuffled the cards. "I don't think they're getting much done, other than mooning around at each other."

Funny Ramona should mention that, because Calla noticed that was pretty much what Ramona and Dad were doing.

Though he did interrupt his flirtation to say, "Calla, don't forget to pack a weekend bag tonight so that I can get it in the morning. We're leaving right from school when I pick you up."

"I will," she promised, and made a hasty escape back up to her room with a healthy snack of crackers, baby carrots, and hummus—along with one of the big chocolate brownies Ramona had baked for Dad.

Well, she claimed to have baked them for everyone. But she was looking at Dad when she said it.

Calla finished her homework, then threw some stuff into her duffel bag for the weekend trip. They're heading first to Penn State in State College, Pennsylvania, then back up to New York State: Cornell in Ithaca and Colgate in Hamilton. The circular route Dad's mapped out will bring them back home late Sunday night.

As she waits for the screen to load, she wonders when she should break it to her father that she's pretty sure she wants to stay closer to home—home, as in Lily Dale—next year. She looked over the brochures Mrs. Erskine gave her, and Fredonia State University seems to offer everything she should probably be looking for.

Not that she's looking for much more than a solid school that happens to be nearby.

Oh, well. She'll worry about all of that later, because at last, her e-mail has popped up on the screen.

Sure enough, there's one from Kevin.

No, not one.

One . . . two . . . three?

Frowning, she opens the most recent.

Okay, now I'm being a pain, I know. But I'm really worried about you. You don't have to write a long note back. Just a quick one to let me know that you're okay. Otherwise, I might show up on your grandmother's doorstep to see for myself. Love, Kevin

Calla sits for a moment with her fingers poised over the keyboard.

Then, her mind made up, she begins typing.

I'm fine. Don't worry.

She pauses.

Should she tell him she and Dad are going to be visiting Cornell this weekend?

No.

She simply types in her name.

It looks funny without anything before the signature.

Anything . . . like *love?*

No way.

She backspaces, erasing her name, then hits Send.

He'll know who it's from.

As she suspected, her in-box contains a few other e-mails. One is from Billy Pijuan, an old friend of hers in Florida, a few are from Lisa, the rest are spam.

She clicks on one of Lisa's.

Come on, hurry up.

It's taking forever. This is going to be—

Suddenly, a screen pops up—and it isn't Lisa's e-mail.

It's a new sign-on screen—and her mother's screen name is already typed into the User ID box. The cursor is blinking like a beacon in the password box.

How did this screen pop up?

Puzzled, Calla wonders if she hit some kind of automated button by accident.

Maybe.

Now that she's here . . .

She finds herself typing in her mother's password.

Then, inhaling deeply, about to hit Enter . . .

She smells it.

Lilies of the valley.

The room is filled with the fragrance.

"Aiyana?" Calla turns in her chair and there she is.

The spirit guide is dressed in flowing white, as always, her black hair pulled back from her lovely, dark-complected face. She nods at Calla, an approving gleam in her almond-shaped black eyes, almost as if . . .

"Did you do this?" Calla blurts, indicating the screen.

Aiyana lifts a hand, pointing at it.

"You want me to read her e-mail," Calla says. "Is that it?"

"Find her."

"Find who? My mother?" Calla asks, but the apparition is fading.

Within moments, she's gone, and so is the scent of lilies of the valley.

Calla looks back at the screen.

She doesn't remember hitting Enter after typing the password, but the mailbox icon has loaded anyway.

With a shrug, she goes directly to the archives, scrolling back to last spring.

She skims past the mail she's already read, and ignores all the correspondence that isn't between her mother and Darrin.

Dear Stephanie, I understand if you can't forgive me, but please forgive yourself. You didn't do anything wrong. Everything is my fault. I'm the one who persuaded you not to tell anyone you were pregnant, because I was a coward. I guess I still am, because I find it much easier to communicate with you this way than I did in person. There are so many things I couldn't say to you when I saw you in Boston.

I guess the most important is that I still love you, and always will.

I'm not the same person I was back then. I had developed a drug habit to help me deal with all those psychic visions I couldn't control—but that made everything even worse. I made stupid decisions because of the drugs. That's not an excuse, it's just the way things were. The dumbest one of all—even worse than leaving you—was telling you the baby had died.

But what, Calla wonders, was the alternative?
Wouldn't Mom have figured that out anyway?
This doesn't make any sense.

When you went into premature labor before we had even figured out what we were going to do with the baby, I pretty much went off the deep end. I had thought from the start that we were both set on giving it up for adoption, but then you started to seem unsure about it. I realized you probably wouldn't be able to go through with it once the baby was born. And I honestly believed it was the right thing to do—for selfish reasons, but also for unselfish ones.

I contacted the agency a few months before the baby was born, without telling you. It was the wrong kind of agency, obviously, and I definitely went about it the wrong way, but I guess I couldn't see past all the money they were offering. Not just to cover expenses, but a big chunk of cash for the baby. I never realized how wrong that was. I never thought to check their credentials and it never occurred to me that they weren't a legitimate operation. I figured that was how it worked. I figured everybody would win—our daughter would grow up better than we could ever raise her, and we could have our lives back.

The pieces are beginning to fall into place, but Calla doesn't dare assume anything.

Breath caught in her throat, she reads on, filled with dread—and with hope.

I made myself believe that I was actually doing you a favor, telling you the baby had been stillborn. I know that seems hard to believe, but I figured you would get over it and move on quicker than you would if you thought she was out there somewhere.

Remember how you kept saying you could have sworn you heard her cry? That almost did me in. I convinced you that you were just out of it from all the pain. I hated myself for that. What broke my heart more than anything was finding that memorial you made in the woods, in the spot where she was born, just so you'd have a grave where you could leave flowers. By then, I wanted desperately to tell you that she was alive, but I was too afraid.

Calla gasps, pressing a fist to her trembling lips as she rereads the last line.

So it's true.

The baby didn't die after all.

I really do have a sister.

A maelstrom of questions fills Calla's head.

She seizes upon the most important one: Where is she?

Please, please let the information be here.

She reads on.

Then, a few months later, out of the blue, you confronted me to ask whether I had been telling the truth
about the baby being stillborn. You gave me a chance to
redeem myself, and instead I lied to you again. That
was when I knew I had to get out of Lily Dale. For good.

Leaving you—and my parents—was hard. But I'm
ashamed to say it wasn't as hard as it should have
been, thanks to the drugs. I had to hit rock bottom in
order to get clean. I had to get used to my psychic
visions all over again, and accept them. That took years.
By that time, I knew I had to tell you the truth. But finding you, and finding the nerve to do it, took years, too.

Anyway, you should know that I've already hired a
private detective to find our daughter. I told him the
whole story, including date of birth and the name of
the agency. I'll let you know as soon as I find out anything more.

Calla hurriedly and shakily closes that e-mail and clicks on
the next. It's from her mother.

Darrin, you gave me a lot to think about. I don't know
what else to say, other than please let me know when
you hear from the detective.

More than two weeks go by without an e-mail between them.

Then comes one from Darrin, dated March 16.

That was the day before he showed up on our doorstep back in Florida with that manila envelope.

They've found her. They even gave me pictures they shot with a telephoto lens. She's beautiful. I've booked a flight to Tampa first thing tomorrow morning so that I can show you and talk about this in person. Let me know if that's okay, and where to meet you. I can be there by 11.

Oh my God, oh my God, oh my God . . .

Lightheaded, breathless, Calla moves on to her mother's terse response.

Just come here. I'll work from home. Jeff will be on campus and my daughter will be at school.

Mom gave him their address.

And he showed up, Calla remembers. But not until that afternoon. The flight must have been late. Calla was already back from school by that time. And Mom wasn't working when she got there—she was baking Irish soda bread, for Saint Patrick's Day.

Mom always puttered in the kitchen when she was stressed out. She said it relaxed her.

She burned the soda bread that day, while she was talking to a man Calla believed was a colleague.

Tom Leolyn.

Darrin Yates.

In his hands was a manila envelope.

It was in Mom's hands, too, when Sharon Logan pushed her down the stairs. But it wasn't beside her body when Calla found her.

There's another e-mail from Mom to Darrin, sent a few minutes later. It reads simply,

I forgot to ask—where did you find her? And what's her name?

Darrin's response is even shorter.

In Geneseo, New York. Her name is Laura Logan.

TWENTY

New York City
Friday, October 12
12:08 a.m.

Laura turns onto her stomach and bunches the pillow beneath her cheek, willing herself to fall asleep.

It never works.

Nothing ever has.

She's had insomnia for as long as she can remember. She'd thought it might get better once she left Geneseo.

If anything, it's grown worse.

Every night, she lies awake remembering what it was like to live in that house with the woman she'd grown up believing was her mother.

Then along came a stranger who knocked on the door one day last spring and changed everything.

It was a warm afternoon, and Laura had snuck out of the house to soak up the sunshine, sitting in a lawn chair tucked just behind the front porch. She often sat there on nice days, not wanting to be seen by passersby.

Old habits die hard.

All her life, she had been teased about living in the neon purple house. As if the paint job had anything to do with her.

"It's my mother's favorite color," she would explain, as if that made it better, somehow.

But it beat the truth: that Mother had always believed for some reason that the purple would ward off evil spirits.

She had always been superstitious—not like regular people, who might not walk under a ladder or sit in the thirteenth row on a plane.

No, she was superstitious to the extreme, paranoid about everything—just plain crazy, Laura eventually realized.

That's why she had escaped every chance she got—even if just to sit outside in the sun and pretend, for a while, that she was a normal person living a normal life.

If she hadn't been out there on that beautiful day last spring, she never would have overheard the conversation between Mom and the man who came to the door.

She never would have discovered that she, Laura Logan, wasn't the daughter of a crazy woman and the nameless, face-less man who had supposedly run off and left her mother before Laura was even born.

Her real father was the stranger on the porch.

He introduced himself as Tom Leolyn and said he had given up his newborn daughter to an illegal adoption ring more than twenty years ago. Her real mother had been told the baby hadn't survived.

They were just kids at the time, he said. He hadn't known any better. It had all been a terrible mistake.

Laura sat in stunned silence, listening—and waiting for the inevitable violent reaction from Mother.

Who really wasn't her mother at all.

For Laura, that discovery was the answer to her most fervent prayer—that she would somehow find a way to escape her oppressive existence.

Father Donald, the kindly parish priest in town who had befriended her when she was a forlorn little girl, had always promised that her prayers would be answered one day, if she only had faith.

Faith, and hope. Those were the two things he wanted her to have. She clung to both in all those miserable years of abuse at the hands of a mentally ill woman who should never have been allowed to raise a child.

That, Laura realized as she sat there eavesdropping, must have been why Sharon Logan had resorted to illegal adoption. No one in their right mind would entrust a baby to her.

"I'll need to think about this," she told Laura's real father that day at her doorstep, after a long silence. "Tell me where to reach you."

Laura—who had witnessed a lifetime of ranting fits over the slightest mishap—was shocked by the response.

"I'll give you my phone number," Tom began, but Mother interrupted him.

"I'll take that, and your address, too. So that I know where you are, when it comes time to find you."

It was an odd thing for her to say, Laura thought.

But then, Mother was nothing if not odd.

The stranger gave her his address, somewhere in Maine, and went on his way, and Mother never said a word about it.

Laura waited until Mother left the house to run errands, then searched the house until she found—under Mother's mattress—the papers that proved the stranger correct.

Standing there holding the proof that she had been bought, as an infant, like a piece of livestock, Laura sobbed.

Not sorrowful tears.

Tears of sheer relief.

And the blanket of guilt that had smothered her for as long as she could remember—guilt for not loving her own mother—began to lift at last.

Now it all made sense.

Now she was free to run away and never look back.

She huddles deeper into the blanket, trying to forget what she'd had to do in order to make that happen.

Stealing all that money from Mother was probably wrong.

Probably?

Of course it was.

But it was her only option. She had no money to her own name. Mother demanded that she hand over every cent she earned at the data-entry job she'd been working since high school graduation. Laura had always been well aware that all that cash was hidden around the house. Mother was much too paranoid to keep it in a bank.

When she helped herself to thousands of dollars from the stash, Laura reminded herself that she was only reclaiming what was rightfully hers.

Without it, she couldn't have fled to New York City, found an apartment, bought a decent wardrobe so that she could find work.

Before she left, she went to see her old friend, Father Donald.

"I'm leaving," she told him. "Please don't tell my mother if she asks."

He nodded with understanding. "Where are you going, child?"

"To New York City. I have to get away from her. I just found out—she's not even my real mother."

He raised an eyebrow, but didn't ask for an explanation, and she didn't offer one. The less he knew, the better.

"I just wanted to thank you for all you've done for me," she told him, "And to say good-bye."

He hugged her, then blessed her, praying over her with a gentle hand on her forehead.

She went into the confessional on her way out. It made her feel a little better about stealing the money.

Still, it's bothered her ever since—and not just because of a guilty conscience.

For all she knows, Mother reported the theft to the police. They could very well be looking for her now.

She was convinced Mother herself was looking for her until the day she read about Sharon Logan being jailed for murder in Florida.

That doesn't mean Laura won't be found by the authorities and arrested for stealing the money. Or, at the very least, stripped of the fragile new life she's attempting to build here, three-hundred-odd miles and a world away from Geneseo.

That can't happen.

She can't let that happen.

For the first time, she's living life on her own terms.

Sleep. . . . I need to sleep.

But it's so cold.

Shivering even beneath the weight of two blankets, Laura contemplates getting out of bed to turn up the thermostat. It was already on seventy-two when she went to bed, though. How much warmer can she set it?

The strange thing is . . .

It doesn't feel like seventy-two in this room. More like a good thirty or forty degrees colder.

Curling onto her side in an attempt to use her own body heat for warmth, Laura spots something a few feet away from her.

Not something.

Someone.

A male figure is standing in the shadows near the foot of the bed.

Even as Laura lets out a blood-curdling scream, she recognizes him.

It's her father.

Her *real* father: Tom Leolyn.

Paralyzed with fear, she stares at him.

How did he get in?

What does he want?

Is he here to hurt her?

No. He can't be.

Somehow, she senses that he doesn't mean her any harm.

But that doesn't make it any less disturbing to find someone standing over your bed in the middle of the night.

Summoning every shred of courage she possesses, Laura manages to speak at last. "Wh-what are you doing here?"

"She's looking for you."

"But—she's in jail."

"No." He shakes his head vehemently. "Not—"

The piercing ring of the telephone shatters the night.

Laura instinctively looks toward the receiver on her bedside table.

As she reaches for it, she glances back at her midnight visitor.

He's gone.

How can it be?

She flips on the lamp, looks wildly around the room, leans over the edge of the bed to see if he's dropped to the floor; looks under the bed to see if he's hiding there.

No sign of him.

And the phone is still ringing.

You must have been dreaming. You fell asleep without realizing it, and you dreamed he was here.

Of course.

That makes perfect sense.

Rather, it *would* make perfect sense . . . if she hadn't felt as though she were wide awake the whole time.

Well, that's how it is with some dreams, she reminds herself as she picks up the phone at last. *They seem so real you could swear they actually took place.*

She looks at the Caller ID window. It's a local 212 number.

"Laura, it's Liz," a voice says in her ear. "Are you okay?"

Liz . . . ?

"I heard you scream!"

Oh. Liz Jessee. The landlady.

Her apartment is right across the hall from Laura's.

"I'm fine. I just saw . . . a roach."

"A roach! Oh, no! Please tell me you didn't."

But then Laura would have to come up with some other reason she'd be screaming in the night.

"It's New York," she murmurs. "These things happen."

"Not in *my* building."

As Liz Jessee assures her that she'll send an exterminator to take care of the problem first thing in the morning, Laura looks again at the spot where she saw the stranger who claimed to be her father.

Still empty.

Of course it is.

And, she realizes, the room is comfortably warm now.

Now?

It was always warm.

Of course it was.

Because she dreamed about the chill, and she dreamed about the intruder.

Just as she keeps dreaming about the argument between those two women, and the little Victorian cottages by an unfamiliar lake, and the fragrant white flowers.

TWENTY-ONE

Lily Dale
Friday, October 12
12:33 a.m.

"Goodnight, Odelia. Thanks for everything!" Ramona's voice carries from the front hall up to where Calla sits, knees bent and back against the wall, in the shadows at the top of the stairs.

"I'm the one who should be thanking *you*! If we play poker every night like this, I'll be able to afford a fancy vacation this winter."

"If we play poker every night like this, I'll have to stay in your house while you're on your fancy vacation this winter," Ramona returns with a laugh, "because I'll be living out on the streets."

"I'll be right there with you," Dad says. "I don't know why

I thought it would be a good idea to play poker with a bunch of psychics. All I've got left are the clothes on my back."

"Just be glad we weren't playing strip poker," Andy tells him, "because then you wouldn't even have that."

Raucous laughter floats up to Calla's ears.

Please go. Just go, she silently begs Dad, Ramona, and Andy.

But she's been willing the three of them to leave for a couple of hours now, to no avail. They all had a grand old time down there playing cards while Calla paced her room, quietly freaking out about what she discovered in her mother's e-mail.

She has a sister.

In Geneseo.

Illegally adopted at birth.

Her name is Laura Logan.

Psychic skills are hardly required to figure out that there's some connection between Laura and Sharon Logan and the purple house.

From the rest of the e-mails exchanged after Tom came to Florida to show Mom the photos, Calla learned that he had gone to Geneseo himself a few weeks later. There, he had spoken to the adoptive mother, Sharon, who had seemed receptive to putting him and Mom in touch with their daughter, now grown.

> I didn't get to see her, but I'm sure I will, eventually.
> We both will. I told her adoptive mother where to
> find me.

Those words ring ominously in Calla's head.

Sharon Logan had found him, all right.

Found him—and killed him.

At last, Calla hears the front door close and lock in the hallway below. She leans over and peeks around the newel post at the top of the stairs.

Her grandmother is standing at the door, parting the window curtain to watch the others leave. After a few moments, she reaches for the wall switch and flicks off the porch light, then the hall light.

"Gammy?" Calla calls, as she turns toward the stairs to start up.

Odelia gasps. "Calla! You scared the life out of me!" She rests a hand against her rib cage.

"Sorry."

"What are you doing up? It's a school night, and you have a big trip coming up tomorrow with your dad."

"Gammy, I need to talk to you."

Her grandmother peers up at her. "Are you crying? Is something wrong?"

The answer to both questions is yes, but Calla can't seem to find her voice.

"Calla?" Odelia hurries up the stairs toward her. "What happened?"

"Tell me the truth about something, Gammy. Please."

"What is it?"

"My mother had a baby, and you knew about it. You knew Darrin told her the baby had died, and that he'd thrown the body into the lake."

Odelia goes absolutely still, and paler than Calla has ever seen her.

"Say something, Gammy. Say that I'm right. Say that you knew."

Odelia sinks onto the top step, shaken. "I did know."

"She told you?"

"No! No, she never told me, and I was fool enough never to realize. I knew Stephanie had put on weight, but that happens to a lot of kids, and she hid it so well I convinced myself it was just a few pounds. And I knew she'd been much quieter than usual, but I blamed that on her boyfriend. He was a bad influence from the start. So much negative energy."

"Because he was on drugs?"

"Probably." Odelia shrugs. "All I knew was that I didn't want my daughter around him. And the more I told her to stay away, the more she wanted to be with him."

"How did you find out about the baby?" Calla sits beside her.

"The way I find out a lot of things. Visions."

"What do you mean?"

"I kept seeing Stephanie cradling a baby in her arms. At first I thought it was a premonition. But then I started to realize it had already happened."

"How?"

"I just knew," Odelia says simply. "I confronted her. I asked if she had been pregnant. She told me that she had, months earlier, and that the baby had been stillborn. She said Darrin had put the remains in the lake."

Choked by a sob, she can't go on.

"He lied, Gammy." Calla, too, is crying. "He lied about that. The baby didn't die."

"What?" Odelia widens her teary eyes. "How do you know?"

"I found an e-mail he sent to Mom. He said—"

"I knew it! I knew that baby was alive! I tried to convince Stephanie. I told her to go to the police. She refused. She said Darrin would never have done something like that to her, but I think she knew, deep down inside, that she was wrong. A mother knows in her gut whether her child is alive or dead. Sometimes, she just might not want to see it or believe it, but she knows."

Calla remembers Mrs. Yates's grief-ravaged face and nods mutely.

"I told Stephanie to look into it, anyway, for her own peace of mind. But she had promised Darrin she'd never tell a soul about the baby. So I told her to confront *him*, at least. Ask him if the baby really had died. She didn't want to do that, either."

"She did do it, though, Gammy."

"How do you know?"

"She wrote about it. She asked him, but he lied again. And he left Lily Dale not long after that. Do you remember?"

Odelia nods sadly. "He broke Stephanie's heart. I tried to convince her that she was better off, but I couldn't get through to her. Eventually she left, too. Went away to graduate school, met your father, got married, moved to Florida, had you . . ."

"You used to visit us when I was little."

"Yes."

"Then you had an argument with Mom. About the baby. After all those years."

"I can't believe you remember that, Calla. You were so young."

"I do. I remember and I . . . I dream about it sometimes."

"About the argument?"

"Yes."

"It was a bad one. I should never have brought up the baby to Stephanie after all that time had gone by. But every now and then, I would still have a dream. I just always had the feeling that I had another grandchild out there somewhere. I told your mother to look into it again, but she refused. I don't know if she was still trying to protect Darrin, or if she was trying to protect herself, or you and your father."

Odelia wipes tears away with the bell-shaped sleeve of her pumpkin-colored top.

"You told Mom that you thought the lake should be dredged, didn't you, Gammy? To find the baby's body."

"Yes. She got so angry with me. Mind you, I really didn't think they'd find anything. I had spent all those years living on the shore of the lake. I think I'd have sensed whether my own flesh and blood was buried in it."

"But you told me never to set foot in that water."

"Because . . ." Odelia shudders. "There was always a chance I could be wrong. Even now, every time I look at that lake, I wonder."

"But you don't have to wonder anymore. The baby lived and she was illegally adopted, Gammy—by Sharon Logan."

It takes a moment for the name to register. When it does, Odelia gasps.

"She killed Darrin," Calla goes on, "after he showed up on her doorstep asking about the adoption. Then she killed my mother, too. And then she came after me."

"We have to tell the police."

"I know. But Gammy, I'm afraid to tell them—or anyone. Then Dad will find out about everything."

"He deserves to know the truth, Calla."

"It's going to hurt him."

"Maybe not. Maybe he'll be glad to know that Stephanie lives on in another daughter—and that you have a half sister."

"I doubt that."

"Don't underestimate him." Gammy touches Calla's cheek. "How about you? How do you feel about all of this?"

"About having a sister?" Just saying the words out loud sends a little jolt through her.

A sister.

She actually has a sister.

"I don't know how I feel," she tells her grandmother. "I mean, I guess I won't, until I find her and meet her."

"Do you know anything about her?"

"Her name is Laura."

"That's a pretty name."

It is. *Laura.*

"Like the former first lady."

Laura Bush.

Suddenly, she realizes something.

"Gammy, that day at Ramona's—"

"I know. I just remembered." Her grandmother nods. "That magazine that flew off the table in the guest room—"

"Laura Bush was on the cover."

"Yes. That was no accident." Her grandmother shakes her head. "Spirit could have been a little more specific."

An image flashes into Calla's head as she speaks.

She sees a young girl wearing a calico dress and sunbonnet:

Laura, from the Little House books Calla read and loved as a child.

Pieces begin to fall into place.

The same books are on the shelf in Mom's room upstairs.

That image of Mom lying on her bed reading one of them.

Even the dream Calla had about being on an airplane and seeing a pioneer girl standing on top of a tall building.

"We need to call Detective Lutz," her grandmother decides.

"When? Now?"

"It's the middle of the night. I think it can wait until morning."

"But . . . what about school? And my trip with Dad?"

Her grandmother looks at her for a long time. "Your life is going to change again, you know. When all of this comes out. You're going to want to find your sister, or she's going to want to find you—or maybe not. I don't know."

"I don't, either." Suddenly, Calla is nervous about what lies ahead. "I was kind of just looking forward to a normal school day tomorrow, and going away with Dad."

"Then that's what you should do," Odelia says firmly. "I'll speak to the detectives after you leave. We'll let them do their thing. Then when you come back, you'll have had more time to get used to all of this, and you'll know what you want to do about it."

"You mean, about finding my sister." At her grandmother's nod, Calla asks, "Why wouldn't I want to find her? She's my own flesh and blood."

"Mine, too. But we have to remember—she had a very different life. She might not even be aware that she was adopted. There's a chance she'll want nothing to do with us."

"You're right." Calla sighs. "What about Dad?"

"We have to tell him," Odelia decides, "before we go to the detectives. He deserves to know."

"Can you tell him, Gammy? Tomorrow, when I'm at school? Please?"

Her grandmother seems to be weighing the decision. Then she nods. "All right. I'll tell him."

"Thank you."

Calla leans her head on her grandmother's shoulder and closes her eyes as Odelia strokes her hair.

Laura.

I have a sister.

TWENTY-TWO

New York City
Friday, October 12
7:20 a.m.

"I don't understand, though," Geraldine says on the other end of the telephone. "What was so wrong with the place that you don't want to go back there even for a day, to finish out the week?"

Laura clutches the receiver hard against her ear, pacing. "There was nothing wrong with it. It just wasn't . . . right. For me."

Because "she's looking for me," according to my midnight dream visitor. And after that hang-up phone call yesterday, she might have found me.

But of course, she can't say that to Geraldine.

Or to anyone.

"Will you call me if another assignment comes in this morning?" she asks Geraldine.

"Sure."

No, she won't, Laura realizes as she hangs up. *She thinks I'm too picky. Or worse yet, just plain old lazy. She doesn't know me at all.*

Then again . . . who does?

She desperately misses having a confidante—someone with whom she can share the whole truth, and be herself.

Father Donald is the only person in her life who ever fit that role, and now he's hundreds of miles away.

Maybe you can make a friend here in New York, she tells herself, feeling homesick.

The trouble with temp work, though, is that it's hard to create a social life around the people you meet. Just as you get to know them, it's on to a new assignment.

How else is she supposed to meet anyone?

There's Liz Jessee. She's certainly friendly, interesting—and, in return, *interested.* She asks far too many questions for Laura's comfort. Anyway, Liz is an older married woman, with a family and a busy life of her own.

I just don't fit in here, Laura tells herself wearily.

I don't fit in anywhere.

All her life, she wanted to be like the other girls, the ones she saw through the windows of the purple house: skipping rope, riding bikes, walking to school in groups of two and three.

Mother home-schooled Laura, of course, and never let her out to play with the other kids when they were brave enough to knock on the door and ask. Which happened maybe two or three times in Laura's entire childhood.

The buzzer on the wall sounds loudly, jarring her from this dismal trip down memory lane.

Stop feeling sorry for yourself, she scolds as she goes over to the intercom. *A lot of people are lonely. You'll get over it. Someday, things will be different.*

But there are tears in her eyes, and a lump in her throat refuses to subside as she presses the Talk button. "Who's there?"

"I have a delivery," a female voice responds.

At this hour of the morning?

"Sorry, you must have the wrong apartment."

"No . . . it's for Five B."

Laura has been in the city long enough to have developed some street smarts. She isn't expecting anything, and for all she knows, it's a scam for her to let a would-be thief into the building.

"I don't think so," she says into the intercom, and steps away from the door.

A few seconds later, it buzzes again.

She tries to ignore it, but uneasiness settles over her. If it is a would-be thief, it's one who's determined to target Laura. Otherwise, she'd have moved on to someone else's buzzer.

But maybe she has, Laura decides, when a full moment of silence has gone by. That, or maybe she's gone on to try a different building.

Then she hears some kind of movement in the hallway outside her door.

Heart pounding, Laura steals over to the peephole and peers through just in time to see the back of a woman's head disappearing toward the stairway.

She waits a few seconds, then opens the door a crack, leaving the chain on, just in case.

There, on the mat, is a vase filled with gorgeous white flowers.

Calla lilies, she realizes, unchaining the door and reaching down to pick up the vase.

There's an envelope stuck to a pronged plastic fork in the bouquet, and she opens it with trepidation.

Who on earth would be sending her flowers?

Inside the envelope, instead of a florist's card, there's a folded piece of 8½ by 11 white paper.

Opening it, she's startled to see that it's a paid voucher for an airplane ticket from New York City to Rochester, just north of Geneseo. It's for a flight tomorrow morning—and the passenger name is Laura Logan.

What on earth?

Puzzled, she hurries back over to the window and peers down at the street.

After a few moments, a figure emerges from the front door of the building. It's the same woman Laura just glimpsed in the hallway. She's dressed in some kind of long white dress and wears her jet black hair in a bun.

After descending from the stoop to the sidewalk she pauses and looks directly up at Laura's window.

Her face is exotically beautiful and completely unfamiliar. But there's something so warm and reassuring in the smile she beams at Laura that Laura can't help but return it.

She quickly opens the window and sticks her head out, calling, "Excuse me!"

But somehow, the woman is gone.

She couldn't have stepped into a cab—there aren't any in sight. Laura cranes her neck to look up and down the street, but she's nowhere to be seen. How on earth could she have walked away so quickly?

"Hi, Laura!" Liz Jessee, holding her broom, steps into view on the stoop.

"Liz! Did you see where she went?"

"Who?"

"The delivery woman."

"What delivery woman?"

"From the florist. She just left me flowers." And a plane ticket.

Which isn't the only odd thing that's happened lately.

"When did she leave them?"

"Just now."

"Now?" Liz echoes. "But . . . it's so early."

"I know. Did you see which way she went when she came out of the building?" she asks again, trying not to sound impatient.

"I didn't see anyone come out of the building," Liz tells her. "I've been here for the last ten minutes, sweeping the front vestibule."

"But . . ."

"Laura, are you okay? You look a little pale."

"I'm just . . . feeling under the weather," she says slowly. "I think I'll go lie down."

"Oh . . . the exterminator is coming at nine o'clock sharp. I hope that's not a problem."

"Exterminator?"

"For the roaches. Last night. Remember?"

Oh. Right. The roaches.

Which don't exist.

Just like the man at the foot of her bed, who didn't exist.

And now the floral delivery woman, who also doesn't exist.

Laura tells Liz that'll be fine, closes the window, and turns around, wondering what she'll find.

Who knows? Maybe she imagined the flowers and the ticket home, too.

Of course she did.

Everyone knows florists don't deliver airline vouchers.

Except . . . this one does.

Because the voucher—and the vase filled with beautiful white lilies—calla lilies—is definitely real.

TWENTY-THREE

Lily Dale
Friday, October 12
7:25 a.m.

"Lisa! Thank goodness you didn't leave for school yet!"

"Calla?" On the other end of the telephone line, her friend sounds bewildered. "What are you doing calling so early? Is everything okay?"

"Not really."

"Oh, no. What happened?"

Where to begin?

She sinks into a chair at her grandmother's kitchen table.

Maybe it was a mistake to call Lisa right now. She did it impulsively, as she was getting ready to head out the door to school. Odelia is still asleep upstairs—Calla checked several times as she was taking a shower and getting dressed and using makeup in an attempt to mask the evidence of her rough, sleepless night.

Knowing Evangeline left for school early today, she found herself feeling desperate to talk to someone.

I guess I just have to say it out loud, Calla decides. *To make sure it's really true.*

Which really makes no sense.

She knows it's true.

She was up all night, reading and rereading her mother's computer files.

"The thing is, Lis' . . . last night, I found out that I have a sister."

"What?!"

"Yeah. I know. Crazy, right?" She gives a shaky, humorless laugh.

"What are you talking about? How can you have a sister?"

"It's a half sister, really. My mother had a baby with her old boyfriend."

"You have a baby sister and she didn't tell you? But how—"

"No! No, this was years ago. Before she even met my dad. It's not a baby sister, it's a grown-up sister. Half sister."

"I can't believe this," Lisa drawls.

"I can't, either." Calla toys with the strap of her duffel bag, packed for the weekend and draped over the back of the chair, ready for her grandmother to deliver to Dad later . . . along with the bombshell discovery.

"Did you meet her?"

"No! I didn't even know she existed until a few hours ago." Calla draws a deep breath. "She was actually adopted by Sharon Logan."

"Who's that?"

"The woman who—"

"I just remembered! That horrid woman?"

"Yes."

"This is unbelievable, Calla. I can't . . . I just don't know what to say."

"You don't have to say anything. I just needed to call you."

"I wish I was there."

"I wish you were, too," she says miserably, trying hard not to start crying again. It's bad enough for her to be going to school today with circles under her eyes from lack of sleep. Red and swollen eyes from fresh tears will make people ask questions.

"Do you want me to call Kevin and ask him to drive over from Ithaca?"

"What? No!" That's the *last* thing she wants.

"He'd want to be there for you, Calla. He's really worried. And he said you never answered any of his e-mails."

"I just did, last night."

And he should have been there for me months ago. Now it's too late.

"Really? You haven't answered any of mine."

"I know, I'm sorry." Suddenly, she feels so weary she can barely speak.

It was probably a mistake to call Lisa. She can be so . . . needy. And right now, Calla is too needy herself to be there for anyone else . . . let alone deal with an ex-boyfriend.

Yes, Kevin and Lisa—and their parents—were there for her and Dad last weekend, in Florida.

Yes, Calla welcomed their support. Even Kevin's.

But now that she's back in Lily Dale . . .

There are just some things they will never understand.

"Lisa, you know what? I've got to run or I'll be late for school."

"Okay. . . . I'll call you this afternoon."

"Okay. Wait! Don't. I'll be gone."

"Where are you going?"

"To look at colleges with my dad."

There's a pause on the other end of the line. "You mean, around there?"

"In Pennsylvania, and . . . around New York." She doesn't want to mention Cornell. In fact, she doesn't even want to *go to* Cornell.

"What about down here?"

"We were just there, and . . . we can't drive there in a weekend!" She tries to make light of it.

"So you're not going to apply to schools with me, like we said?"

This is not a conversation Calla wants to be having now, in the midst of everything else that's gone on.

"Lis', I don't know for sure where I'm going to apply. But . . . I mean, Florida has some bad memories for me, and it's so far away."

"New York is so far away," Lisa returns, "from me. We always had plans to go to college together."

I had a lot of plans that aren't going to work out, Calla wants to tell her. *You can never really count on anything, because your whole world can shatter in an instant.*

But Lisa doesn't get it. She doesn't yet realize that nothing in life is guaranteed.

"You know I love you, Lisa, and I miss you every single day. And no matter where we end up next year, we'll always be friends. You know that, right?"

"Yeah, I know that." But her voice sounds hollow. "I have to get to school now, too. I'll talk to you after the weekend."

"Definitely. Bye, Lis'."

"Wait, Calla? About the other thing? I'm happy for you— that you have a sister. You always wished you weren't an only child. Remember? We used to pretend we were sisters."

She smiles sadly. "I remember."

"I wish—"

"Lis', you're still like a sister to me. Like I said, we'll always be friends."

Friends living separate lives, a thousand miles apart.

Unless I really do decide to go back down south.

She hangs up the phone, pulls on her jacket, and picks up her backpack. As she steps out into the crisp morning, with a hint of sun filtering through red and gold autumn leaves, she knows in her heart that Florida is behind her for good.

TWENTY-FOUR

Lily Dale
Friday, October 12
3:20 p.m.

Stepping through the big double doors at the school's main entrance with Jacy at her side, Calla immediately spots her father, parked in his rental car at the curb.

She can't see his expression from here.

But he knows.

She can feel it. Her grandmother told him everything while Calla was in school, just as Calla asked her to.

Jacy reaches for her hand and squeezes it. "Are you going to be okay?"

Is she?

"I don't know. This is hard."

"Yeah. I know."

Earlier, between classes, she pulled him aside and told him everything. Evangeline, too.

In a way, it felt good to let out the last of her deep, dark secrets. But then, Jacy and Evangeline aren't directly impacted by the news that Mom had a baby—and perhaps, a secret lover—and that Calla has a long-lost sister.

Dad is definitely impacted.

"I kind of wish we weren't going away together for three whole days," she tells Jacy. "It's like there's no escaping any of it."

"There probably wouldn't be if you stayed here, either."

"True."

"But I wish you weren't going away for three days, too."

"Please don't tell me you're having another vision of me in danger."

"No. I'll just miss you."

Her heart skips a beat. "I'll miss you, too."

Looking up at him, Calla wishes everything and everyone— the noisy school, the people, her father and his car, the weekend ahead—could just fall away, leaving her alone with Jacy. Judging by the look in his eyes, he's wishing the same thing.

He leans in and kisses her—not the way he wants to, she senses, and not the way she wants him to—but in a way that's appropriate for broad daylight, at school, with her father in the vicinity.

"You better get going."

"Yeah." She sighs. "Good luck at your track meet later."

"Thanks."

He gives a wave and heads off down the hall toward the boys' locker room.

Reluctantly, Calla walks down the steps through a cold drizzle. As she reaches for the car door handle, she lowers her head to check her father's face through the window.

It's not tear-stained, to her relief. He looks normal. Serious, but normal.

She climbs in. "Hi, Dad."

"Hi, Cal'." He pulls away from the curb, past the waiting line of yellow school buses. "Put on your seat belt."

She does, wondering if they're still going away for the weekend now that he knows. She doesn't want to come right out and ask. What if she was wrong and he doesn't know? What if, for some reason, Gammy decided not to tell him?

"Dad? Did you remember to pick up my overnight bag?"

"Got it."

"Good."

How is she going to bring up what happened last night? What if he doesn't?

What if she has to wonder all weekend whether—

"Calla, I had a long talk with your grandmother this morning. And with Detective Lutz and Detective Kearney."

Oh.

Okay, then.

He knows.

She takes a deep breath, glad he's driving so they don't have to look each other in the eye. "Was it about Mom?"

"Yes, and the first thing I want you to know is that I'm okay. You don't have to worry about me. I can live with this. All right?"

"Are you sure?"

"Positive. Was it easy to hear that Mom kept something

this big from me for all these years? I won't lie to you. It wasn't. But I'll survive, and so will you. And now, maybe we'll get some answers."

"Did you tell the police?"

"Yes."

"What did they say?"

"They wrote down everything and they said they'll look into it." He shrugs. "They had already been trying to locate Sharon Logan's daughter, Laura, from what I understand."

"You mean they already knew she was Mom and Darrin's baby?"

"No! No, they didn't know. They wanted to talk to her about Sharon."

Suddenly, it hits Calla.

Wanted to.

Trying to locate.

"You mean . . . they can't find her?"

"No. Not yet." Dad hesitates. "She, uh, seems to have gone missing a while back."

"Missing!" Calla's heart sinks. "What if something's happened to her, too? What if—"

She can't even say it. She rests her head miserably against the passenger window as her father turns left onto Route 60, heading north toward the Thruway.

Is it possible she's found her sister only to lose her again . . . this time, forever?

"Calla? Do you have a feeling one way or another? About Laura being dead or alive?"

Caught off guard by her father's question, she turns slowly to look at him.

"What do you mean . . . a feeling?"

Dad is focused on the road through the windshield. "I mean, your grandmother thought I should know everything. Not just about Mom. About you, too."

"You mean . . . ?"

"I mean I know you have a—what do you like to call it around here? A gift?"

"More like . . . an ability." Her heart is racing. "It doesn't always feel like a gift."

"I can imagine. And I understand why you didn't tell me."

"You do?"

He nods. "I'm going to try to be more open-minded from now on. I'm tired of secrets, and I think you are, too. What do you say we make a fresh start? Starting today?"

"Okay. Starting today."

"No more secrets. Agreed?"

She hesitates only a split second, wondering if she should tell him about her mother and Darrin maybe having an affair behind his back.

But is it really her place to do that?

No. It's not. At least, not right now.

You're not a hundred percent sure.

Ninety-nine-point-nine percent, based on the evidence, but . . .

"Agreed," she tells her father, with a twinge of guilt.

"Good. And in that spirit—no pun intended—I have a suggestion."

"What?"

He hesitates, and glances over at her.

"What?" she repeats, sensing that *everything* isn't behind them.

"What do you say we go visit your grandfather in Pittsburgh?"

"When?"

"No time like the present. We're already headed for Pennsylvania."

"But . . . what if he doesn't want to see us?"

"That's a chance we'll have to take. Are you game?"

Calla nods slowly. "I'm game."

TWENTY-FIVE

Pittsburgh, Pennsylvania
Friday, October 12
7 p.m.

The address Odelia wrote down for Calla and her father is located in a hilly, working-class neighborhood on the south side of Pittsburgh.

The two-story white house itself is pretty basic—two windows upstairs, two down, and a door in the middle. No porch, ornate woodwork, or flower garden like the ones in Lily Dale. In fact, the only thing this one has in common with the cottages there—besides being over a century old—is that it could use a paint job.

As Calla and her father head up the front walk in the dark, she fights the urge to run back to the car. They rehearsed what they're going to say. Dad is going to do most of the talking—or all of it, if she can't find her voice.

"Are you sure you want to do this?" he asks her as they climb the steps.

No. But she sees a curtain part at the window beside the door.

Too late to back out now.

"I'm sure."

He rings the bell, and Calla braces herself to meet her grandfather.

But it's a woman who turns on the outside light and answers the door.

She's stocky, with gray hair and a tired, weathered face.

"Are you Mrs. Lauder?" Dad asks.

"Yes."

"Is Jack at home?"

"Yes."

"Can we please speak to him?"

"About what?"

"About . . ."

Dad hesitates. He doesn't want to say anything about Jack having a daughter, Calla realizes. Just in case his wife doesn't know.

"Tell him it's about Lily Dale."

"Lily Dale," the woman repeats. She looks at Calla. "And that's you?"

"Um . . . what?"

"You're Lily Dale?"

Oh! The woman thinks it's a person's name, not a place. Which means Jack, just like Mom, wanted to put his life there behind him when he left, not even telling his spouse about it.

Dad answers for Calla. "No, her name is Calla, and I'm Jeff."

The woman nods and closes the door, saying, "Wait here."

Calla hears the click of the lock inside and looks at her father.

"You can't be too careful these days," he tells her.

Less than a minute later, the door opens again.

This time, a man is standing on the threshold.

Calla's grandfather.

Knowing Odelia as she does, she never pictured Jack Lauder to be quite so . . . elderly.

He's of medium height but slightly stooped over. He has very little hair, but what's there is pure white. His face was once handsome, but is now trenched with deep wrinkles.

"I'm Jack Lauder," he tells Dad, and shifts his eyes—hazel, and startlingly familiar—to Calla.

She sees his bushy white eyebrows shoot up, sees the unmistakable flash of realization in his eyes. But he says nothing more.

"I'm Jeff Delaney, and this is my daughter, Calla."

The old man nods.

"We came here from Lily Dale, New York."

Another nod.

Then, "How did you find me?"

Dad hesitates. "Is your wife . . . ?"

"She's in the kitchen." He steps outside and pulls the door closed behind him.

"We found you through Odelia, your . . ."

"Ex-wife." He doesn't ask how Odelia found him. But then, he knows her. Maybe he's not surprised.

"Yes, your ex-wife. And my mother-in-law."

The man looks from Dad to Calla, as if calculating the connection.

Then, softly, he says, "You're Stephanie's daughter."

For the first time, she manages to speak. "Yes."

"You look like her." He swallows hard. "And Stephanie? Where is she?"

Calla and her father look at each other.

"She passed away," Dad tells Jack Lauder gently. "I'm sorry."

A sound comes out of the man—not a moan, not a sigh, not a sob, but some combination of the three, and it sends chills down Calla's spine.

"I—we—thought you should know."

Jack Lauder nods sadly and bends his head, gingerly lowering himself onto the step.

Somewhere in the distance, sirens wail and a fire truck honks its guttural horn. A gust of wind kicks dry leaves against the concrete steps.

Yet again, Calla remembers what Ramona said about the bond between parent and child.

Maybe that's only true when the parents are psychic. Maybe Mom's father had no idea that she was no longer on this earth.

Seeing him wipe a tear from his eye, Calla finds that her sympathy for him is tainted by a flicker of anger.

"Why did you leave?" she hears a voice ask—and realizes, to her shock, that it's her own. She didn't mean to bring that up, especially at this moment, but she can't seem to help it. She's been waiting a long time to find out the answer to that question.

Jack looks up. "Why did I leave?"

The words seem to hang heavily in the air.

"I've asked myself that very question every day of my life," Jack Lauder says at last, "and I think I know why I haven't been able to answer it until now."

"Why?"

"Because I don't like the answer. I don't want to face the ugly truth about myself."

Dad sits on the step beside him. "What is it, Jack?"

"That I couldn't accept the woman I married. I loved her, but I couldn't accept her, or the things that went on around her. I guess I wasn't man enough to handle it. I was afraid."

"A lot of people are afraid of things they can't understand," Dad points out.

"Maybe. That's no excuse. I took a vow, and then I broke it. Ran away. What kind of man runs away?"

Calla thinks of Darrin.

Then of Mom, who twice in her life was abandoned by men she loved.

No wonder she didn't want to tell Dad where she'd come from. She was afraid of losing him, too.

Seeing the look on Dad's face, Calla realizes he's thinking the same thing—and forgiving Mom.

"So what happened, exactly? One day, you just woke up and couldn't take it anymore and decided to leave?" Calla asks her grandfather.

"Not exactly. One day I woke up and found my little girl talking to someone who wasn't there."

"What do you mean?" Calla asks, as an incredible thought takes hold somewhere in the back of her mind.

"Stephanie was having a conversation with someone only she could see. . . . That used to happen a lot, but I tried to ignore it. Told myself a lot of kids have imaginary friends. But that day, as I was watching Stephanie, I saw a chair pull itself out from her little table, like someone had just sat down in the spot where her imaginary friend would be. And I realized . . . it wasn't an imaginary friend. She was seeing ghosts, too."

Wide-eyed, Calla and her father look at each other.

"But Mom . . . she wasn't . . . I mean, she wasn't like her mother," Calla protests, unable to grasp what Jack Lauder is telling her. "She didn't have the ability to—"

"Yes, she did. At least, she did when she was a little girl."

"How can you know that?" Dad asks.

"I know what I saw with my own eyes. And I know what Stephanie told me. I marched over there and I demanded to know who she was talking to, and she said it was a ghost named Miriam. What kind of kid makes up a name like Miriam?"

Calla feels as though the wind has been knocked out of her with a baseball bat.

"I yelled at her," Jack says, wiping tears from his eyes again. "I yelled at my baby girl for something she couldn't help. I told her to cut it out. Stop making things up. She said she wasn't making things up. Then I told her . . . I told her she was nuts. Just like her mother." His voice breaks. "I'm so ashamed."

Sick inside, Calla can't find a thing to say that won't just make it harder on him.

He was wrong to say what he said, to do what he did. So, so wrong.

Because of him, Calla realizes, Mom denied who she really was—not just to the rest of the world, but to herself.

That's why Mom was so upset when she realized I had the ability, too, when I was younger. That's why she told me never to tell anyone, not even Dad.

"I've spent every day of my life regretting that," Jack Lauder tells Dad and Calla, shaking his head. "So many times, I wanted to go back to my wife and daughter . . . but how could I? By the time I figured out that I loved them the way they were, too much time had passed. I missed it all. I missed everything."

"But you remarried," Dad points out.

"Yes. Don't get me wrong—I love my wife. We've had a good life together. Better than I deserved. But I never forgot what I left behind." He pauses. "Did Stephanie . . . did she ever mention me?"

"Just that you left," Calla tells him honestly. "And that it really hurt her."

Understatement of the year.

"I'm so sorry," Jack says again. "And now I'll never have the chance to tell her."

"No," Dad says. "It's too late for that."

"But it's not too late to tell my grandmother."

Jack Lauder looks at Calla, startled.

"No," he agrees thoughtfully, "it's not too late for that."

"Maybe some closure would be good for everyone," Dad says.

"Where would I find Odelia?" he asks. "If, someday, I wanted to talk to her?"

"Same place she was when you left her."

"How is she?"

"She's great," Calla says fiercely, not wanting him to think Odelia has been wasting away since he left.

Jack nods. "I'm not surprised. I knew she'd land on her feet. I'm sure she was better off without me."

How can he say that? Calla wonders. Maybe it's the only way he can deal with what he did.

It seems like lately all she's done is listen to the adults in her life admit that they're flawed; that they've made serious mistakes.

Things were a lot easier back when she believed that growing up meant you were wise, and always knew what to do, and did the right thing.

"Thank you for coming," her grandfather says, painstakingly hoisting himself up off the steps. "I wish I could ask you to stay, but my wife . . . she doesn't know about any of this. Yet."

"Yet?" Dad echoes. "Does that mean you're planning to tell her?"

"Yes. I'd like to get to know you, and my granddaughter. I just need time to make things right here. I hope you understand that."

Dad nods and shakes his hand as Jack says, "Thank you for telling me about Stephanie."

Then Jack turns to Calla, holding out his hand. She hesitates before clasping it.

Instead of shaking it, he puts his other hand around it and squeezes. His grasp is surprisingly strong, and warm.

"I'm sure you did your mother proud, young lady."

Tears spring to her eyes, and she swallows hard, unable to speak.

"I hope we'll meet again." He releases her hand.

"So do I," she manages to say before her father puts an arm around her and, together, they walk through the darkness toward the car.

TWENTY-SIX

New York City
Saturday, October 13
7:05 a.m.

The first rays of sunlight bathe Laura's studio apartment in a soft pink glow as she zips the top of the ancient leather suitcase she found several months ago in the attic of the purple house.

Now, once again, she's packed it with all her worldly possessions—everything she brought with her to New York, plus the few outfits she managed to buy while she was here.

Looking around the room, she wonders if she'll ever see it again.

Maybe not. Maybe there's really nothing for her here in the city after all.

Perhaps it was merely a good place to get lost for a few

months. A good place to figure out that she can survive on her own, here—or anywhere, really.

Maybe there's nothing for her in Geneseo, either, but she can't keep looking over her shoulder for the rest of her life.

It took her all night to figure that out, tossing restlessly and looking, every so often, over at the vase of calla lilies on the bedside table.

She still has no idea who sent them.

Liz Jessee is the only guess that remotely makes sense, but why wouldn't she own up to such a sweet gesture? Anyway, she has no idea that Laura is from western New York. If she were to surprise her with a ticket home, it would be to Minneapolis.

So it couldn't have been Liz.

Who else is there?

Father Donald.

Except, she hasn't been in touch with him since she left. He wouldn't know where to find her.

Laura picks up her suitcase and heads for the door.

The only thing that's certain is that she has a paid seat on a flight leaving New York City in just a few hours.

If she doesn't use it, she might not have another chance.

TWENTY-SEVEN

Ithaca, New York
Saturday, October 13
2:15 p.m.

"Please feel free to ask me any questions you might have," the perky female student guide invites the group at the conclusion of a soggy campus walking tour of Cornell.

Dad looks at Calla beneath their shared umbrella. "Any questions, Cal'?"

She shakes her head. "No. Not really." Other than, *Can we leave now?*

Not just because—lovely and impressive as the university is—she's certain she doesn't want to come here.

But also because she's worried she's going to run into Kevin.

Especially now that he knows she and her father are here today.

This morning, when she and Dad called Odelia to check in, she reported that Kevin had called for her the night before.

Lisa must have told him the latest news. Calla had figured she would.

She hadn't expected him to call, though—much less for her grandmother to tell him where they were.

"I'm sorry—I felt like I should mention it," Odelia said over the phone, to Calla's dismay. "In case you ran into him on campus, or something."

"It's okay," she murmured.

After all, Kevin did offer to show her and Dad around if they came to see Cornell.

She feels guilty for not letting him know they were coming, but she could barely think straight in the days before the trip.

He gave Odelia his dorm phone number—and his cell, too, as if Calla doesn't already have it—and told her to have them call him.

Calla couldn't bring herself to do it.

She doesn't want to see him.

What are the odds that she'll run into him, in the space of a few hours, on what she just learned is an almost eight-hundred-acre campus populated by twenty thousand students—not to mention the countless spirits she's seen wandering everywhere?

Slim to none.

Still, Calla won't breathe easy until they're back in the car and headed to Hamilton, where they'll tour Colgate University tomorrow morning, the last stop on the tour.

They didn't get into State College last night until after ten o'clock, but Dad insisted on driving her through the Penn

State campus before heading to their hotel. This morning, they took an early-bird tour before driving almost three hours to Cornell, arriving just before the day's last scheduled tour started at one o'clock.

"Well, it's been great meeting you all," the guide tells the small group of prospective students and their parents, "and I wish you luck, whether you wind up at Cornell next year or not."

Not, Calla thinks as the group disperses.

If she's learned anything today, it's that she doesn't want to be this far from home. The mountains and gorges of central Pennsylvania and New York State are scenic—breathtaking, even—but she misses Lily Dale already.

Enough that she's certain heading to Colgate will be a waste of time.

No, she's anxious to get back home and wait—or at least, hope—for word on her sister. Gammy said the detectives have had no luck finding Laura Logan so far, but they're searching.

"Are you hungry?" Dad asks as they leave the information center, heading toward the visitors' parking lot.

"A little." She idly watches a group of ghostly students in 1950s-style poodle skirts, bobby sox, and high ponytails cross their path.

"Why don't we go to lunch somewhere in town before we head out to Hamilton?"

"Dad, about that—"

"Calla!"

Startled to hear a male voice shout her name, she spins around.

Kevin.

TWENTY-EIGHT

Geneseo, New York
Saturday, October 13
2:55 p.m.

Filled with misgivings, Laura steps off the bus in Geneseo at last.

Her flight was delayed for hours due to heavy rains sweeping western New York. As she sat endlessly waiting by the gate at JFK airport, it was all she could do not to turn and leave the airport. The only thing that stopped her was the fact that she had already checked her bags, and she knew the plane wouldn't be able to take off without her on board to go with her luggage.

Now that she's here, though, she desperately wishes she hadn't come.

She's desperately tired, and desperately hungry, and after paying the bus fare, she has less than five dollars to her name.

Not sure what will greet her when she reaches the purple house—but certain the fridge contents will be spoiled and the cupboards bare as usual—she decides to stop at the Speakeasy Café first. She might just barely be able to afford a cup of coffee and something small to eat.

Stepping into the warm, cozy room, with its exposed brick walls and battered hardwood floors, Laura is comforted by the strong, welcoming scent of coffee and baked goods. The small, round café tables are filled with college students, none of whom give her a second glance. That's fine with her. She heads for the counter, with its colorful chalkboard menu, and does some quick math. Yup. If she buys coffee and a muffin, she'll have about twelve cents left over.

Then what?

Then you'll figure it out, she tells herself. *One step at a time.*

She waits on the line, pretending to be absorbed by the television set mounted on the wall: breaking news on CNN. There's been a catastrophic earthquake today in Shanghai.

Watching the footage of traumatized people being pulled from the rubble, Laura feels as though she can relate to them: her world has been shaken to the core, and nothing is familiar.

"Well, look who's back in town." The tattooed, heavyset female cashier behind the counter eyes her suitcases.

"Hello," Laura says politely, trying not to panic.

Just because the woman, who happens to be a longtime neighbor on her block of Center Street, has noticed that she's been away doesn't mean—

"I heard about your mother."

Oh, yes it does. Well, of course people know. Being arrested for murder is big news. National news. How could Laura have fooled herself for one instant into believing that the people of Geneseo aren't buzzing?

The cashier, with sympathetic eyes, leans closer to Laura and whispers, "The cops have been in here looking for you."

"When?"

"A few times. Most recently, last night. A coupla detectives from Florida. They've been asking for you all over town, I heard. They said it's real important that they talk to you, and they asked me to call them if I saw you. Now, I can pretend that I didn't, if you want to make yourself scarce again . . . but you might just want to get it over with. Sooner or later, they'll catch up with you, and if you've got nothing to hide . . ."

"I don't," Laura tells her, surprised by her kindness—and her offer. "Do what you have to do."

The woman nods. "You poor thing. Is there anything I can do to help you?"

Conscious of a pair of coeds who have come up behind her, waiting to order, she says, "No. Thank you, though."

"Okay. What can I get for you, then?"

Her appetite is gone, but she has to eat something. Once she gets back home, she's not going to venture out again for a long, long time. "Can I please have a coffee and a corn muffin?"

"Sure. Large or small on the coffee?"

Again, she counts the bills and change in her hand. "Small," she says reluctantly.

The woman fills a large cup, anyway, and puts several

muffins into a white paper bag. "Here," she says, "it's on the house. You just take care of yourself."

Her eyes tearing up, Laura gratefully takes the bag. For the first time, she dares to think she might just be okay here after all.

TWENTY-NINE

Ithaca
Saturday, October 13
3:07 p.m.

"Why don't you two sit here and finish eating," Dad suggests to Calla and Kevin, standing and picking up his tray containing an empty soda can and white paper plate stained orange with pizza grease, "and I'll take the car down the road and gas up for the trip."

"I'm actually just about finished," Calla tells him quickly, not wanting to be left alone in the cozy little pizzeria with Kevin.

He reaches out and touches her hand. "Stay, Calla. I really want to talk to you."

Feeling helpless, she shrugs.

"I'll be back for you in about ten minutes," her father says, and heads out the door.

It was his idea to take Kevin with them for lunch. The two of them carried on a stilted conversation, small talk about college life at Cornell, as Calla halfheartedly nibbled at her pizza.

The strange thing is, as much as she didn't want to run into Kevin . . .

It's kind of comforting to see him.

Scary-comforting.

"Look, I figured you didn't want to see me today," Kevin tells her, pushing away his half-eaten second slice of pizza.

"Was it that obvious?"

"Pretty much." He gives an uncomfortable laugh. "I mean, here you are, right here on campus, and you didn't call me."

"I'm sorry."

"I guess I shouldn't have waited around the information center, checking out all the tour groups coming through today, but I really wanted to talk to you."

"It's okay. I know I should have told you I was going to be here today, but . . ."

But I really couldn't deal with seeing you again.

"You've had a lot going on," he fills in for her. "I know. Lisa called and told me. I didn't want to bring it up in front of your dad."

"About my half sister? My dad knows."

"I wasn't sure. How do you feel about it?"

"Glad. Upset. Scared to death." Kind of how she feels about seeing Kevin again.

"Your grandmother said that they haven't found her yet."

"No."

"What are you going to do when they do?"

"I'm not sure. Meet her, I guess."

"It'll be weird for you to suddenly have a sister after all these years, you know?"

"I know."

"But maybe it'll be nice. You know . . . like a link to your mom."

"Yeah." Calla smiles faintly, folding and unfolding her cold pizza on the plate. "That's what I'm thinking."

"You know, it's strange to see you and your dad without your mom around. I really miss her."

Touched, Calla looks up and is surprised to see tears in Kevin's blue eyes.

"She always made me feel so good about coming to school here," he tells Calla. "You know—like she was really proud that I got in."

"She *was* proud of you," she tells him, wiping at tears in her own eyes with the corner of an unused napkin. "You know her. Ivy League was her thing."

Like Lisa, Kevin might not have as much in common with her daily life now as her new friends do—but he grew up with her. He knew the old, carefree Calla, before her world fell apart. He knew her mother. Jacy and Evangeline and the others didn't. Kevin feels her loss in a way they never will.

You can't just write him out of your life, Calla tells herself. *As hard as it is to accept the way he hurt you, you can't erase all those years—or the feelings you still have for him.*

Maybe it's not love anymore, not the kind a girlfriend has for a boyfriend, anyway. Maybe it's the kind of love you feel for a good, true friend. Maybe that's all she and Kevin were ever meant to be.

"You know, Calla, your mom would have loved to know that you're thinking of coming here, too."

Calla nods. "Except . . . I'm really not."

"You're not?"

"No. I don't want to be this far from home."

He's obviously disappointed. "So you're going back to Florida, then, for school? I mean, my sister will be thrilled, but—"

"No, I mean home, in Lily Dale."

"Really?"

She nods. "I can't go back to Tampa, Kevin. Too much has happened there—and here. I think I want to stay put for a while."

"I know. Seeing you there, when I visited . . . it was like you already belonged, even though . . ."

"Even though what?"

"Even though they all . . . I mean, they go around talking to ghosts, right? That's what Lisa told me."

She's getting tired of defending Lily Dale. "It's not like that."

"What's it like?"

"You wouldn't get it." And she doesn't feel like explaining.

"Try me."

She raises an eyebrow. "You really want to know?"

"I really want to know."

So she tells him. The whole story. Including the part about her own newfound abilities.

When she's finished, Kevin isn't sitting there looking

skeptical or spooked, and he doesn't call her—or her grandmother and her new friends—a bunch of freaks. He's just . . . intrigued.

"So, these spirits that you see . . . are they all around us?"

She glances around the pizzeria. In a nearby booth, she sees a 1940s-era G.I. cuddling his girlfriend, who has pompadour bangs and dark lipstick. In another, she sees a grunge musician–type in a flannel shirt and combat boots. And hovering behind the busboy is a worried sixty-something woman—his grandmother, probably.

"Yeah," she tells Kevin. "They're all around us."

"And you see them all the time?"

"Sometimes I have to look for them. But other times, they're there whether I want to see them or not. I'm trying to learn how to tune them in and out."

"They're teaching you that in Lily Dale?"

"Yes."

"You should stay, then. It sounds like you're in the right place."

"I am. And there's a state university a few miles away. I'm hoping I can go there next year."

"Does your dad know that?"

"No. But I think I'd better tell him."

THIRTY

Geneseo
Saturday, October 13
3:16 p.m.

Walking slowly toward Center Street, Laura can hear church bells ringing, as they do every hour on the hour.

Is it four already?

Surprised, she checks her watch.

Nowhere near four.

That's strange.

Even stranger, she feels compelled to head in their direction, toward the church in the heart of town.

Father Donald.

She needs to see Father Donald.

She covers the few blocks to the church in just a few

minutes, and goes directly to the side door . . . then pauses, frowning.

The stained-glass window—her window, the one that led her here all those years ago—is gone.

It's been replaced with a regular one.

Why?

Maybe someone broke it, she decides as she rings the bell. *I just hope they can find another one just like it.*

It takes Father Donald much longer than usual to come to the door.

When it finally opens, though, for the first time ever, he's not the one who answers it.

An unfamiliar woman stands there, wearing a housekeeper's apron. "Yes?"

"Hi. I was wondering if Father Donald is in?"

"Whom?"

"Father Donald," she repeats, wondering if the housekeeper is new here.

Still, no matter how new, you'd think she'd know the name of the parish priest.

"Father Donald?"

"Yes. Father Donald." Maybe she's hard of hearing.

For a long moment, the woman just looks at her.

"Come in," she says at last. "Have a seat."

Laura perches on a chair in the waiting room, her luggage at her feet, and wishes she hadn't come. There will be plenty of time for her to see Father Donald now that she's back.

The housekeeper reappears. "Follow me," she says tersely. "You can leave your bags there if you like."

Laura does, gladly. They're so heavy, she's dreading carrying them up Center Street. And now that she's detoured here, she'll have even farther to go.

"Here she is, Father," the housekeeper announces, and gestures for Laura to step through an open doorway.

But the priest who greets her in the small study is a stranger. He's a much younger man, with dark curly hair, and he's wearing street clothes—jeans and a long-sleeved polo shirt.

Laura looks around for Father Donald, but doesn't see him anywhere. The room is spartan, with a few tables and chairs, blinds on the windows, a crucifix and some framed pictures on the walls.

"Hi," says the young man. "I'm Father Luke."

"Hi. I'm Laura."

"Why don't you sit down?" He gestures at a wingback chair and sits in one opposite her. "I understand you're looking for Father Donald."

"Yes."

"I'm sorry, Laura, but he passed away."

She gasps in horror. No. Oh, no. Please, no.

Looking confused, Father Luke reaches out and touches her hand. "I didn't mean to upset you. You couldn't have known him, so I didn't think—"

"Yes, I knew him. When?" Laura manages to ask. "When did he die?"

"A long time ago, but—"

"Over the summer?"

"The summer!" The young priest looks startled. Then he gestures up at the wall behind him. "You're talking about Father Donald, right? The one who was once the parish priest here?"

247

Laura looks up. Yes, there he is, smiling down from a portrait, wearing his familiar black shirt and collar.

"Yes. Father Donald," she agrees, hardly able to grasp that she'll never see him again.

"Laura, like I said, you couldn't have known him. He died more than thirty years ago, before you were even born."

THIRTY-ONE

Ithaca
Saturday, October 13
3:17 p.m.

"Maybe I'll drive over and visit sometime," Kevin tells Calla as he gives her a hug, standing on the sidewalk beneath the pizzeria's dripping awning.

"That would be nice," she says, and means it.

"Good-bye, Mr. Delaney. It was good to see you again."

"You too, son."

Calla watches Dad and Kevin shake hands.

Everything happens for a reason.

She's here today not because she needed to see the campus in order to rule it out, but because she needed closure with Kevin. She needed to realize that there might be a place for him in her life after all. Not as a boyfriend—or even as an ex-boyfriend—but as a friend.

Now she needs closure with her father.

"Calla, pull the map out of the glove compartment, will you?" he says as they climb into the car. "I want to see which way to go to get to Hamilton."

"Dad—about that . . ."

He looks at her. "You don't want to go, do you?"

"To Hamilton? No, Dad. I don't. Not today, and not for college. And I don't want to go here to Cornell, either, even though I know how much Mom was hoping for Ivy League for me. Or to Penn State."

Her father nods, seeming to absorb all that.

"Are you mad?"

"Mad? No! I just don't know how to help you figure out what you want to do, Calla. Your mother was so good at this sort of thing. I know I'm the one who's an academic, but I just don't know what to tell you."

"You don't have to tell me anything, Dad. I already know what I want to do. I want to live in Lily Dale, and go to Fredonia State."

"Really?"

"Really."

He seems to be thinking it over.

"It's a good school," he says at last. "I like the idea of having you close by."

"Close by? You mean . . . you're thinking of staying in Lily Dale, too?"

He nods. "Not in Ramona's guest room, though."

"But you're . . . getting along with her. Right?"

"Right!" he says enthusiastically. "We're getting along great!"

She can't help but smile. "I noticed."

"You're sure you don't mind, Calla? Because you've been awfully quiet lately."

Yes. But not because of her father's new relationship.

"Why would I mind, Dad?"

"Maybe it's too soon for you to see me spending so much time with a woman who's not your mother. But, Calla, your mother and I . . . we were living separate lives toward the end. If it weren't for you . . . I don't know that we'd have still been together."

"But . . . that's so sad."

"Your mother and I loved each other very much. But we were never a perfect match. It took me a long time to realize that. When we met, got engaged, got married—it was a whirl-wind. Maybe a little too much of a whirlwind. You know your mother. She always liked to have a plan."

"You mean getting married was her idea?"

"It was *our* idea, but I remember being dazed that this beautiful, successful, amazing woman wanted a guy like me. It was too good to be true. Now, looking back, I think she wanted me because I was safe, you know—after all she'd been through."

"I know she loved you, Dad."

"And I loved her. But I think we both eventually realized that we didn't have a whole lot in common other than being your parents."

"Dad . . ." She hesitates, then voices the question that's been on her mind all weekend. "Did Gammy tell you about . . . Mom and Darrin? I mean . . . about this past spring?"

"Yes. She did. Look, Calla . . . I don't know what was going on between the two of them, but whatever happened, I have to forgive your mother. And so do you."

"I'm trying."

"I hope you'll try to forgive me, too."

"Forgive *you*? For what?"

"Nothing is ever all one person's fault, Calla. If the marriage was failing . . . we were both responsible. The other thing is, I shouldn't have gone off to California in August and left you to deal with everything on your own, in a strange place—and I mean that in the most literal sense."

But not in a bad way, she realizes, seeing the affectionate smile on his face.

"I wasn't on my own, Dad. I had Gammy."

"Yes, and she's been great. And I guess I was just so devastated by what happened that I couldn't think clearly. But now that the fog has lifted, I know that you and I belong together."

"In Lily Dale."

"For now, yes. For a while, at least. But I can't stay with the Taggarts forever. I figured I could look for a place to rent, and see if I can get a teaching position."

"What if you don't? I mean, right away?"

"I won't have to worry," he levels a look at her, "if I sell the house. But I don't know how you feel about that."

"Sell it, Dad."

"Are you sure?"

"Positive."

It will mean cutting their last real tie to Tampa.

But that, Calla realizes, will be a relief.

It's time to move on.

"All right, then. I'll get the ball rolling on that. I was worried about how you were going to take it."

"It's just a house. And you can probably get a lot of money for it."

"Let's hope so."

"I could never live there again, after what happened there. With Mom, and then with me. Every time I saw that stairway, or the pool, I'd remember all the bad stuff. And I just want to forget."

"So do I." He puts the keys in the ignition. "I guess that's all decided, then?"

"All decided."

"So we're going home to Lily Dale now?"

"Yes," she says with a smile, settling into the passenger's seat. "We're going home to Lily Dale."

THIRTY-TWO

Ithaca
Saturday, October 13
8:31 p.m.

The drive home to Lily Dale has been far more pleasant than the outbound trip. Calla and her father haven't done much talking, but their silence is companionable. Now that there's a sense of resolution for their future—as a family, and as individuals—the tension between them has all but dissolved.

It's almost like the old days.

Almost . . . but not quite.

Things will never be the same. Mom is gone, and Calla is growing up, and Dad is moving on, with Ramona.

Calla's excited about what the future might hold for her, but a part of her might always feel wistful for the past.

Maybe that's how it's supposed to be. Maybe that's how it is for everyone. The older you get, the more memories you've made. You can't help but think about the way things used to be.

Especially when you've lost someone you love.

Darkness has long since fallen by the time Calla and her father arrive at the Lily Dale gates.

"Your grandmother is going to want to hear everything," Dad comments as they drive along the rutted, deserted street.

"About . . . Jack?" Calla can't bring herself to call him her grandfather. Not aloud. Maybe someday, but not yet.

"About Jack, and about your decision to stay here for college."

Calla nods. Odelia isn't the only one who will want to hear that.

"Dad? Do you think you could drop me off at Jacy's?"

She fully expects him to protest, but he nods. "That's fine. Just don't stay long. It's getting late, and it's a school night."

"Thanks, Dad."

She's about to tell him how to get there but he's already making the turn in the right direction.

"You know where Jacy lives?" Calla asks in surprise as they pull up in front of Walt and Peter's house.

"Sure. What do you think I am, an outsider?"

Calla can't help but grin at that. Dad, too, has become a part of this strange little town. Who would have ever guessed that would happen? Who would have guessed any of this?

"Thanks, Dad." She leans over to give him a hug. "For dropping me off here and for . . . everything."

"No problem. Don't be long," he reminds her as she climbs out of the car. "Your grandmother will be waiting to hear all about it, and she'll want to hear it from you."

Calla waves and hurries toward the porch, hoping Jacy will be home. She's never just dropped in before, but . . .

It's okay, right? He's her boyfriend, after all.

Warmed by the thought, she hurries up the steps and rings the bell.

It doesn't take long for the front light to flick on. In Lily Dale, even in the off-season, people are quite accustomed to doorbells ringing unexpectedly.

Balding, bearded Peter Clifford opens the door, probably expecting a walk-in appointment for a reading.

"Calla!"

"Hi, Peter. I'm sorry to just barge in but I wanted to talk to Jacy if he's home?"

"No problem, he's upstairs taking a shower. Come on in." Peter holds the door open.

She steps into the entryway and admires the decor, as always. Peter and Walt have painstakingly remodeled the old cottage with authentic Victorian wallpaper, fixtures, and furnishings, capturing the period style without frilly, fussy overkill.

Peter calls to Jacy from the foot of the stairs. "Are you out of the shower? Calla's here!"

"What? Really? Tell her I'll be down in two seconds!"

"He'll be down in two seconds," Peter echoes dryly. "How's your grandmother? I haven't seen her in a few days."

"I haven't, either," she admits. "I've been away, looking at colleges."

"Really? Where?"

She tells him, and his eyes light up.

"I went to Cornell. I was premed. Of course that was way back in the olden days."

Peter, she knows, used to be an M.D. Somewhere along the way, he made the transition to psychic healer and wound up in Lily Dale.

"So are you applying there?" he asks Calla.

"To Cornell?" She shakes her head. "I want to stay close to home."

"Jacy will, too. I wish we could afford to send him away to school, but . . ." He shrugs.

Calla—who hasn't been able to get much out of Jacy when it comes to talk of next year—is glad to hear that he won't be going far. Absence doesn't always make the heart grow fonder, she acknowledges, thinking of Kevin.

Footsteps creak down the stairs and Jacy appears. He's barefoot, wearing gray sweats, and his hair looks as though he just rubbed it dry with a towel.

"Hey, what are you doing here?" He seems pleasantly surprised to see her. "I thought you weren't coming back until tomorrow night."

"I wasn't, but . . . here I am."

She wonders if Jacy's going to hug her in front of Peter. Nope. He stops short a few feet away, but shoots his foster dad a pointed look.

"I'll be in the other room," Peter announces, and disappears discreetly.

Jacy immediately puts his arms around Calla. He's so

familiar and comfortable, and she rests her cheek against the soft, plush cotton of his sweatshirt, inhaling the pleasant scent of laundry detergent and shampoo and toothpaste.

"Why'd you come back? I hope you and your dad didn't have a big blowout."

"No, it was kind of . . . the opposite." She tells him about their conversation, then about the encounter with Jack Lauder, and finally, about her decision not to go away to school. She leaves out the part about Kevin.

Maybe she'll share that with Jacy later. Maybe she'll keep it to herself.

"I'm really glad to hear that, Calla. I know it's almost a year off, but . . . I hate thinking about you leaving."

"Really?"

"Yeah, really." He rests his forehead against hers. "What, you think I want to be apart from you now that we've finally figured things out?"

Her heart is beating like crazy. "I don't want to be apart from you, either. I mean, that's not why I'm staying here—it's not the only reason, is what I mean, but—"

"Stop talking, Calla."

"What? Why?" she asks, dismayed by his terse tone.

"Because when you're talking, I can't kiss you."

"Oh! I thought you were—"

"You're still talking," he murmurs, and then his lips brush hers and she melts against him, glad to be home where she belongs.

THIRTY-THREE

Geneseo
Sunday, October 14
3:00 p.m.

"We appreciate your talking to us, Miss Logan."

Laura nods, watching the portly Detective Lutz set aside the notebook in which he wrote down everything she said to him and his partner, Detective Kearney, in the last hour.

"There's just one last thing we need to discuss now."

Her heart sinks.

All she wants—all she's wanted since they contacted her yesterday afternoon, not long after she arrived home, shell-shocked, at the purple house—is to get this business over with. Only then can she move on.

Move on . . . to what?

Okay, so she has a lot to figure out.

Starting with the fact that she apparently experienced an ongoing hallucination for most of her life.

Maybe I'm crazy, just like Mother.

Things like that run in families.

Only, she isn't my family.

The whole thing would be easier for her to accept if Father Donald had turned out to be an imaginary friend—someone she totally made up.

Instead, he turned out to be someone who actually existed . . .

Long before she was born.

Someone she never heard of.

How can she possibly explain that?

It doesn't make sense.

Maybe it will, somehow, when she's past all this other business involving Mother's incarceration for murder.

No . . . not "Mother."

She's not my mother.

The police confirmed that Sharon Logan illegally adopted Laura as an infant, from a teenaged couple named Stephanie Lauder and Darrin Yates. They confirmed, too, that Stephanie hadn't been aware of the adoption, or even that it had been a live birth.

The detectives also delivered the shocking news that Sharon Logan murdered both Stephanie and Darrin. The motive is unclear.

But Laura, remembering Sharon's constant paranoia and all the irrational talk about someone taking Laura away from her, can only guess that the woman's worst nightmare had come true the day Darrin showed up on her doorstep. Sharon thought the truth would come out and she would lose Laura forever.

Never mind that Laura was already an adult.

In her delusional state, Sharon didn't seem to realize Laura had grown up.

Ironically, now Sharon Logan really has lost Laura forever.

She's not the only one facing a loss.

Not only is Laura's so-called mother not her mother—but her real parents, who, just months ago, were almost within her grasp—are now dead.

Apparently, it was her father's ghost that Laura saw that night in her apartment.

Unless you dreamed it.

What about Father Donald? Did she dream him, too? Every single time? Even when she saw him in broad daylight?

Yet, if she did dream him . . . that doesn't change the fact that he really did exist.

I never heard of him, though.

It just doesn't make sense.

Dreams . . . ghosts . . .

What's the difference? They're both intangible.

Either way, it doesn't change the fact that there's no chance of a fairy-tale ending for Laura. No chance of finding her long-lost family and living happily ever after.

Sharon Logan robbed her of that, too.

If you look hard enough, you can always find it.

No.

No, you can't.

Now what? she wonders, seeing the detectives look at each

other, then back at her again across the dusty coffee table in the living room of the purple house.

"Laura, your mother—Stephanie, your birth mother—had another child. Later in life, when she was married and living in Florida."

Another child . . .

"She's living now with her grandmother and her father in a town called Lily Dale, about a two-hour drive from here."

"Who is?" she asks, unable to register the meaning.

"Your half sister."

Her half sister.

She has a half sister?

"Her name is Calla. She looks a lot like you. She's seventeen years old. She wants to meet you."

Laura has a half sister.

She looks a lot like Laura.

Her name is Calla.

She's seventeen years old.

And, Laura realizes, she's the girl Sharon Logan attacked in Florida.

"She . . . wants to meet me?" she echoes as the pieces fall into place at last. "Why?"

Again, the detectives exchange a glance.

"I guess it's only natural," Detective Lutz begins, "for her to want to—"

"Blame someone for what happened to her, and to her mom?"

"I don't think that's why," Detective Kearney tells her. "You're her sister."

Laura swallows hard. *My sister. I have a sister.*

I'm not alone in this world after all.

But what if . . .

What if Laura agrees to meet her, thinking she'll finally have a family after all—only to find out that Calla does blame her for what Sharon Logan did?

Who needs that?

There's an uncomfortable silence.

"I'm sorry. I just . . . I can't."

"Why not?"

If you look hard enough, you can always find it.

No, you can't.

You can't find hope, or faith . . .

You can't even find the man who made that promise, because he doesn't exist.

Laura gets shakily to her feet. "Tell her that I can't. Please."

Detective Kearney hands her an envelope.

"What is this?"

"Her contact information. In case you change your mind. You never know."

For a moment, Laura considers handing it back.

But Kearney is right. You never know.

Standing here in the quiet, empty house, facing an uncertain future without a friend in the world—this world, anyway—Laura tucks the envelope into her pocket.

"We'll be in touch again to follow up," Lutz tells her as she ushers the detectives to the door.

She shrugs. "I'll be here."

"Are you sure?"

"Where else would I be?"

"Thank you for your time."

"You're welcome."

Both detectives shake her hand, and then they're on their way, leaving Laura alone on the porch of the empty purple house.

THIRTY-FOUR

Lily Dale
Monday, October 15
12:48 p.m.

On a blustery day like today, Calla is certain she'll find Jacy in the cafeteria, and she's right.

There he is, sitting in a corner with a book and a brown bag sandwich.

Yesterday, they spent the whole afternoon together. He took her to a movie, and then out to Rocco's in Fredonia for chicken wings. The date was a welcome reprieve from sitting around at home waiting for the phone to ring.

They still haven't heard back from the detectives, and Calla has been trying to accept the fact that her sister might never be found.

"I have a feeling you're going to meet her, though," Evangeline insisted on the way to school this morning.

"I wish I had that feeling," Calla replied wistfully. "How is it that I can get premonitions about some things—things that don't matter at all—and have no clue about what's going to happen in my own life?"

"You know why, don't you?"

Calla nodded. She did know, only too well, that intense emotion can act as a barricade to block a medium from seeing things about her own life.

Now, as she heads for her usual table, her heart sinks when she sees Sarita there alone, eating a pear, her dark, close-cropped head bent over an open textbook.

"Hi, Sarita. . . . Where's Willow?" Calla had seen her in school earlier today, in first-period health class, red-eyed and withdrawn.

When Calla asked her about her mother, she said simply that Althea is still in the hospital, and she hurried away to her next class.

Sarita looks up, and her dark eyes are troubled. "She was called out last period. I'm not sure what happened, but someone saw her leaving school with her jacket and backpack."

"Oh, no."

Calla has a flash of Willow in a hospital room—frightened, crying over a sheet-draped corpse in the bed.

"I'm sure it was about her mom," Sarita says.

Calla nods, but doesn't mention what she just saw.

There's always a chance it was her imagination, and not an actual vision.

Even though I know it was real.

"Did you study for the chemistry test this afternoon?" she asks Sarita.

"A little. I'm nowhere near ready. Nothing like cramming at the last minute."

"I'll leave you alone, then," Calla says, glad for the excuse to make her way over to Jacy after all.

"Thanks. Wish me luck."

"Good luck. Let me know if you hear anything more about Willow."

Jacy looks up as she approaches him, smiles, and pulls out the empty chair beside him.

She puts down her tray but doesn't sit. "Listen, Jacy . . . did you by any chance drive to school today?"

Sometimes, in bad weather, his foster dads let him take one of their cars.

"Yeah," he says. "I did. Why?"

"I have to ask you a huge favor. And you can totally say no."

He smiles faintly. "Can I totally say yes, too?"

"I hope you do, but . . . it could get you into trouble."

"What is it?"

"I need a ride down to Brooks Memorial Hospital in Dunkirk."

"I'll wait here," Jacy whispers, touching Calla's arm as they step off the elevator in a hushed hospital corridor.

"Are you sure?"

"I don't think she'll want to see me at a time like this."

"I'm not sure she'll want to see me, either," Calla says uneasily, wondering if it was a mistake to come.

And not just because she's cutting her afternoon classes to be here.

It's not as though she and Willow are old friends, or even particularly close friends, in the grand scheme of things. After all, Calla's barely known her for two months, and Willow is the kind of person who keeps others safely at arm's length.

But back at school, pure instinct kicked in and this seemed like the right thing for Calla to do.

Now . . .

Not so much.

"She needs you," Jacy says simply, and squeezes Calla's hand.

"Me? But I'm—"

"Look, she needs *someone*. And you're the only one who knows what she's going through. Go ahead."

Calla takes a deep breath and starts down the corridor toward Althea York's room. Nurses, orderlies, and doctors stride past her in both directions. She half expects someone to stop her—half wishes someone would—but no one gives her a second look.

Medical personnel aren't the only ones here.

There are spirits, too.

They're everywhere, all ages, from all walks of life. Some are wearing hospital gowns, others wear street clothes from another era.

Glancing into one room as she passes, she sees a wizened elderly man lying motionless in a bed, yet also standing beside it, staring down at his body as a gray-haired woman weeps over it and a priest gives last rites.

He looks up, catching Calla's eye, and flashes her a broad grin.

He's happy, she realizes, startled. He's dying . . . or has just died . . . yet he looks like he's just won the lottery.

Unnerved by the strange sight, she moves on to Althea's room, footsteps slowing as she nears the open doorway.

She stops just short of it, hearing the steady beeping of medical monitors and muffled sobbing.

I can't do this.

Willow is about to lose her mother. Who is Calla to barge in there in some misguided effort to comfort her?

Her own pain is still so raw that she can feel hot tears springing to her eyes and emotion clogging her throat. Like Willow needs this.

"There you are."

She looks up, startled to hear a voice directly beside her.

A woman is standing there, wearing a white nurse's uniform and cap and the kindest smile Calla has ever seen.

Puzzled, Calla looks over one shoulder, then the other, assuming the nurse is talking to somebody else . . . but the spot behind her is empty.

"Are you . . . talking to me?"

The nurse nods. "We've been waiting for you to get here, Calla. She needs you."

"Who does?" She must be mistaken, thinking she's talking to somebody else.

But she said my name . . .

How does she know my name?

"Willow . . . Althea's daughter. You're her friend. Go

269

ahead . . . go hold her hand. Be with her. We've been waiting," she says again.

Calla swallows hard, wipes at her teary eyes with her sleeve, and forces herself to cover the last few steps to the threshold.

There, she hesitates and looks back to ask the nurse how she knew Calla was coming.

The spot where she stood is empty.

Doctors, orderlies, and nurses continue to bustle up and down the corridor. But the nurses are wearing green scrubs.

Not old-fashioned white uniforms with caps.

Slowly, she turns back toward the room.

Althea's large form is lying in the bed covered with a white sheet drawn up to her chest. She's connected to beeping machines through a series of tubes. Her breaths are coming harshly, with a long pause between each one.

Willow is at her bedside, clutching one of her mother's hands in both of hers, crying softly. In the window, over her shoulder, white confetti is swirling.

It takes Calla a moment to realize what it is.

Snow.

My first snowfall.

For a moment, she stares at it in wonder. Then Willow looks up. "Calla!"

Calla opens her mouth to speak but can't find her voice.

"You're here. . . . I can't believe you're here. Thank you so much."

I do belong here.

She hurries across the room to Willow. "Is she . . . ?"

"Her body is shutting down."

"I'm so sorry."

"They called me at school. It could be any time now."

"Where's your father?"

Willow's eyes harden. "At work. He said he'd try to come by on his lunch hour, but . . . he didn't."

"Maybe he's on his way."

"I don't want to see him. I don't want him to see . . . her." She sweeps a hand toward her mother.

Looking at Althea, Calla is filled with sorrow.

Then she realizes that Althea isn't just lying in the bed. She's standing beside it, too. Looking younger, and healthier, than Calla has ever seen her.

The body in the bed is technically still alive, she realizes— but now it's like an empty house whose residents have packed up and moved on. Althea's soul has already left. She's free.

Their eyes meet, and Althea flashes a radiant smile. "Thank you, Calla."

"For what?"

Willow looks up. "What?"

"What?"

"Did you just say something?"

She can't hear or see her mother, Calla realizes. *She doesn't realize her spirit has already left her body. Should I tell her?*

Remembering how helpless and frustrated she herself felt the long-ago day when Althea saw her own mother and she herself couldn't, Calla decides against it.

Willow is too emotional right now.

"Thank you for being with her, Calla." Althea is bathed in white light now, growing more ethereal by the second. "You'll help her. Take care of her."

She nods, unable to speak for the monstrous lump in her throat.

As she watches, Althea disappears into the light.

In that instant, the beeping gives way to an ominous, steady tone.

"No," Willow sobs. "Oh, Mommy, no."

Calla can only hold her, cry with her, knowing only too well the pain that lies ahead.

THIRTY-FIVE

Lily Dale
Monday, October 15
7:35 p.m.

"How is she?" Odelia asks anxiously, waiting at the foot of the stairs when Calla descends after leaving Willow in her bedroom.

"She said she just wants to be alone."

"That might not be the best thing."

"She needs some time to pull herself together, Gammy." Having been in Willow's shoes, Calla remembers only too well the aching sorrow that makes it nearly impossible to speak, to breathe, to function.

"We'll check on her in a little while. I'm sure her father will be calling to see how she is."

Calla isn't so sure about that.

When Willow's dad showed up at the hospital, he seemed to be all-business, betraying very little emotion even as he gave his daughter a perfunctory hug. He didn't argue when Calla and Jacy offered to take Willow back to Lily Dale with them as he made the necessary arrangements to transport Althea from the hospital to the funeral home.

Willow didn't argue, either . . . although she did ask to go back to her own house. Calla talked her out of it. She couldn't bear the thought of her friend alone there tonight . . . or ever.

Her grandmother puts an arm around her. "How about you, my dear? Are *you* okay?"

"I'm just so sad."

"It's a tragic loss. She was a special lady."

"She was." Calla hesitates. "Um, know what? Before Althea died, I saw her."

"What do you mean?"

As she describes the experience, Odelia smiles and nods.

"That's exactly how it is," she tells Calla. "Like an empty house. The body is just a mortal shell that houses the spirit. Spirit lives on."

If Calla ever had any doubt about that, she doesn't any longer. Althea York lives on . . .

Somewhere.

And so does my mom. I just haven't been able to see her, just like Willow couldn't see her mother today.

It was Althea who told Calla that her own grief might be acting as a barrier to being able to connect with her mother's spirit.

But after a couple of months in Lily Dale, Calla did finally feel her energy—and her touch—in the Yorks' kitchen one night. It wasn't nearly enough. But it was something.

"Come on," her grandmother says. "Let's go into the kitchen and I'll make you something to eat."

They walk, arm in arm, toward the back of the house, with Miriam drifting alongside them.

"I'm worried about Willow, Gammy. What's going to happen to her now?"

"I suppose she'll go live with her father."

"She doesn't want to."

"No, I imagine she doesn't." Odelia's mouth hardens. Obviously, she's encountered Mr. York before.

"I have an idea, Gammy."

"I bet it's the same idea I have."

Calla smiles, relieved. "I love you, Gammy."

"I love you, too."

"So Willow can stay here, with us?"

"Absolutely. If she wants to. And if *you* don't mind. It's going to be close quarters in your room."

"I know. I don't mind. It'll be . . . like having a sister."

"All right." Odelia opens the refrigerator. "We'll talk to her when the dust settles a bit, so to speak. What do you want to—"

The doorbell rings loudly, cutting her off.

"Do you have an appointment coming, Gammy?"

"No. Must be Willow's father or a walk-in reading." She closes the fridge. "I'll go see."

Calla sits at the table and worries about Willow. She's got a rough road ahead, even with support from Calla and her grandmother.

The front door closes and she hears a male voice mingling with her grandmother's in the front hall. Willow's father must be here. Calla hadn't expected him so soon. That's a good sign. Maybe he really is—

"Calla? There's someone here to see you."

She looks up, startled.

How could she have forgotten?

"Calla, I've been channeling your mother for days now," David Slayton announces. "She wants to come through to you."

THIRTY-SIX

Lily Dale
Monday, October 15
8:02 p.m.

"Give me your hands, please."

Calla hesitates, then reaches across the space between her chair and David Slayton's, facing each other in her grandmother's dimly lit back room.

As he takes both her hands in his, she feels a little jolt . . . like an electric shock, transmitted from his fingertips to her own.

Her heart, which has been doing double-time since he showed up in the kitchen a short while ago, beats even faster.

If anyone can bring her mother through to her, it's David Slayton.

Then again . . .

As she watches him bow his head and close his eyes, she reminds herself that his son Blue doesn't seem to have the abilities he claims to have.

But his father's the real deal, Calla decides. He must be, because she can literally feel the room, his body, his hands, teeming with energy.

Perhaps a full minute of charged silence passes. Calla doesn't dare move, speak, even breathe.

Then David Slayton announces, "She's here."

"My mother?"

"Yes."

Calla exhales a shaky breath, waiting, knowing better than to interrupt his concentration with comments or questions.

"She wants you to know that she's proud of you. She says you're stronger and braver than she ever knew. Stronger and braver than you ever knew, too."

David Slayton opens his eyes and his smile catches her off guard. He nods intently, listening to someone whose voice only he can hear.

"She's telling you that the danger has passed. You're safe now. She's saying you don't have to worry about her anymore. Do you understand what she means by this?"

"Yes."

He's talking about Sharon Logan.

Rather, *Mom* is.

Calla can actually feel her mother's presence emanating from the medium, senses the softening in his demeanor as he channels her.

"She asks your forgiveness. Do you understand?"

Again, Calla nods.

"She did what she had to do. She never meant to hurt anyone else. You, above all. For you, there is only love."

"Oh, Mom . . . Mom, I miss you so much. Every day. I feel so alone without you."

"No. You're never alone. You're surrounded by her love. She wants you to remember that."

"I will," she whispers.

"She's saying she wants you to stay close to your family. That you've made the right decision. She says your family will be there for you. Your father, your grandmother, your sister . . ."

Calla's eyes widen. "My sister?"

"She's showing me you and your sister, holding hands. Very much together. Do you understand this?"

"I . . . I'm not sure."

Is he talking about Laura Logan?

Or about Willow, whom Calla just told Odelia might become like a sister if she moves in?

He goes silent, apparently listening. He nods again.

"She wishes she hadn't told you to ignore your abilities when you were a little girl. She's sorry. She was frightened."

"By . . . my abilities?"

Again, he listens. "When she was a child, things went very wrong for her because of her communication with Spirit."

Yes. Her father left.

"She was afraid something similar would happen to you. She asked you to deny who you were. She's sorry," he repeats.

"It's okay, Mom. It's okay. I know why you did it. You only wanted what was best."

279

David Slayton pauses, eyes closed.

"She says she never was true to herself. To who she really was."

"What do you mean, Mom?" Calla whispers into the empty room.

The answer comes in a moment. "She suppressed her own abilities. Didn't want anyone to know. She shouldn't have done that. She should have listened to her guides. If she had, she would have known everything. Do you understand?"

About her baby being alive? Is that what she means?

David Slayton doesn't wait for an answer. His eyes snap open.

"She has an important message for you, and your father, too."

Calla draws a deep breath and sits upright in the chair. "What is it?"

"She says . . . she was true to him. Even though it may appear otherwise. She was true to him until the end. She wants to remind you that caring about someone new doesn't mean you automatically stop caring about someone else you once loved."

Calla recognizes the exact words that popped into her head weeks ago, when she was wondering how she could have lingering feelings for Kevin now that she's involved with Jacy.

That really was a message from Mom.

"And your mother thinks that your father is making good choices now," David goes on. "Does that make sense to you?"

"Yes." Calla exhales in relief. "It does. I'll tell him."

Another long pause.

And then, "She's glad you're aware of your guides. They've

always been a part of you, but you didn't know it. Keep listening to them. Keep watching them. They're there to help you."

"Do you mean . . . Aiyana?"

"And others who will become known to you. Your mother wants you to know that you'll have different guides at different times in your life, to enlighten you as you need it."

Thinking of the phantom nurse in the hospital, Calla smiles faintly, then asks, "Is my mother one of my guides?"

"She's with you. Always."

"Mom, please . . . please, I need to see you." Tears stream down Calla's cheeks.

"*Feel* her."

David Slayton's hands are radiating energy.

"I *can* feel her," she whispers.

But I want to see her. Just once. Just one last time. Please . . .

She clenches David's hands like a lifeline.

Focus.

Tune in.

She isn't sure whether the voice she's hearing is her own, or his, or even her mother's; doesn't know whether the words are only in her head or being spoken aloud.

Tune in.

Tune in.

With every ounce of her being, Calla concentrates on opening herself to her mother's energy, feeding off David's.

Please. . . .

A blurry human shape begins to materialize before her.

"Mom," Calla breathes, as familiar features, so strikingly similar to her own, gain clarity.

Mom.

She's here.

Her mother's hazel eyes gaze lovingly at her.

Her mother's lips curve in a joyful smile.

Her mother's graceful hand reaches toward her, and Calla feels the whisper of her gentle touch against her cheek.

Bathed in the glow of maternal love, she memorizes the moment, memorizes the feel of her mother's hand and the expression on her mother's face, knowing it will have to last her a lifetime.

I love you.

Her mother's voice fills Calla's head.

I'm with you.

Don't ever forget.

"I won't," she promises. "I won't ever forget."

"She's pulling back," David announces, but he doesn't have to say it.

Calla can feel it. Her mother's energy is gone.

"Thank you," she tells David Slayton. "Thank you so much. I've been searching for her everywhere."

He nods, looking satisfied.

Then he asks, "Do you remember what I told you when we met?"

"You told me to keep my wits about me. You said I was in danger. You were right."

"Not that. Do you remember what else I said?"

She does.

Slowly, she says, "You told me that I was gifted."

"Not just gifted. You have tremendous power in your ability—power that's unusual in one so young. You need to learn to use your mediumship for the greater good. It's not always an easy thing to do, even for an adult."

"How am I supposed to figure things out?"

"With the help of others who have been where you are right now."

"Like Patsy Metcalf? I'm taking her class in Beginning Mediumship so that I can—"

"No," he cuts in impatiently, "that's not what I meant. It's a start, but it isn't enough."

"You mean my grandmother?"

"Odelia is descended from a long line of powerful mediums—each generation stronger than the next. What does that mean to you?"

Unsure how to answer, Calla falls helplessly silent.

"You need a mentor whose ability is greater than your own."

He walks to the doorway, then turns back, his eyes boring into hers, watching her as if weighing a decision.

Then he gives a firm nod. "I'll help you."

Shocked, she can't even respond. This is a man who doesn't give his own son the time of day. Why would he want to help her?

"You and I will discuss this further. For now, good night."

With that, he's gone.

Calla sighs and leans back in the chair, spent.

She can scarcely believe what happened here tonight.

She actually got to see her mother, just as she's been yearning to do since she arrived in Lily Dale and discovered that it might just be possible.

One last time. That's all I asked for. That's all I wanted.

But it wasn't enough.

It could never be enough.

David Slayton's words echo in her head.

You have tremendous power in your ability, Calla.

Maybe he's right about that.

Only time will tell.

THIRTY-SEVEN

Geneseo
Tuesday, October 16
3:17 a.m.

The dream is familiar.

Laura walks in the sunshine along a grassy shore beside a beautiful country lake surrounded by rolling, wooded hills. Just ahead are charming Victorian cottages, and there are little white flowers everywhere: lilies of the valley.

She bends to pick one of the bell-shaped blooms and holds it to her nose to breathe in its fragrance.

"Heavenly, isn't it?"

The female voice is familiar. Startled, Laura looks up to see a woman standing beside her, smiling at her with unmistakable love.

Maternal love.

"Mom?"

"I'm sorry, so sorry . . ." Her mother wraps her arms around Laura, holding her. "I never meant to leave you."

"I know."

"But you're not alone. I'm here. I'm always here. And so are your guides. Look for them, Laura." *If you look hard enough, you can always find it.*

Laura doesn't understand . . . and then, all at once, she does.

"Father Donald?" she asks her mother, and her mother nods.

"But I don't feel him. I don't see him."

"You will again."

"I feel so alone, though. Like I don't belong to anyone. I don't belong anywhere."

Her mother lifts an arm and points at the cluster of cottages. Suddenly, they're much closer than they were before. Laura can even see the peeling pinkish orange paint on the one closest to her, a two-story cottage with a front porch.

Someone is there, she realizes. On the porch.

It's her mother—but no, it can't be, because her mother is right here with her, and the person on the porch is too young.

"You're not alone," her mother tells her. "She's been looking for you, Laura."

"Who is she?" Laura asks, though she knows. In her heart, she knows, just as she knew her mother.

"She's your family, and she's waiting."

Laura turns to her mother and sees that she's holding a bouquet of white calla lilies—exactly like the ones she received back in New York.

"Those were from you?" she asks with sudden compre-
hension.

Her mother nods.

"And the plane ticket?"

Another nod.

"But . . . how did you do that?"

"Anything is possible. Anything at all. One day, you'll
understand."

"When?"

"When your own journey on the earth plane has ended
and it's time for you to discover what lies beyond. For now,
Laura, go to your sister. It's time."

With that, her mother is gone, but somehow, Laura knows
everything is going to be okay, because the girl on the porch is
waiting for her.

THIRTY-EIGHT

Lily Dale
Saturday, October 20
11:20 a.m.

Sitting in her Beginning Mediumship class on Saturday morning, Calla is closing her eyes, meditating along with the others, when it happens.

In her mind's eye, she sees herself—at least, that's what she thinks at first.

Then she realizes that the face is a little different, and the hair is a little different, and it's not Calla at all. Nor is it her mother.

It's someone who looks an awful lot like both of them. She's troubled. Frightened. Alone.

"You're my sister," Calla silently tells the girl in her vision. "You're not alone. We have each other, and Gammy, and

288

Mom—she's with us both. Don't you know that? Don't you know that you belong here in Lily Dale?"

The girl smiles then, and holds out something.

Flowers. A bouquet of lilies of the valley.

Calla opens her eyes, and the girl is gone, but the fragrance lingers, all around her. She looks at the others, heads bowed in silent meditation, opening themselves to Spirit just as Calla has.

But I can't stay here, because my sister is waiting.

She doesn't know how she knows that, but she's certain of it.

She quietly rises from her chair and slips unnoticed out into the cold gray autumn day. Wet leaves are slippery beneath her feet, and the drizzle is cold on her cheeks as she hurries toward home. They're predicting snow later. Real snow, not just flurries. This time, it's supposed to stick.

When Calla reaches her grandmother's house, she spots a now-familiar dark sedan parked at the curb.

Detectives Kearney and Lutz are here.

She hurries up the steps and opens the door.

Yes, there they are. She can see them standing in the living room, and her grandmother, and her father, and . . .

The girl glances up, sensing Calla before any of the others realize she's there.

Calla looks at a face that's familiar, and yet not. The girl is troubled. Frightened. Alone.

Calla walks toward her.

"Calla," someone says, "this is Laura. She wanted to meet you."

"You're my sister," Calla tells the girl, just like in the vision—only this time, it's real.

289

And just like in the vision, her sister smiles and holds out something.

It isn't a bouquet.

It's her hand.

As Calla grasps it, she's enveloped by the scent of lilies of the valley.

"Welcome home," a voice says—but it isn't her own.

And it isn't her sister's.

Looking up, Calla sees her mother. *Their* mother.

She smiles, and then she's gone.

But not really, Calla reminds herself. *She's never really gone, and neither is the love.*

If you look hard enough, you can always find it.

AUTHOR'S NOTE

My widowed father still lives in the big old Victorian house where I grew up, though he's lonely there without my mom. Everything is exactly as she left it, right down to the book she was reading—an advance copy of my latest, at the time—her place saved with a bookmark and set on the table next to her living room chair, where she always sat at night and read. She not only lived in the house but died there, too, four years ago this spring. It was on her birthday that April that the doctors told us there was nothing more that could be done to treat her breast cancer. She passed away a few weeks later, two days after Mother's Day.

This past April, my father returned home after a few weeks away to a very strange phenomenon. After it had gone on for a few days, he called me and told me about it.

"Do you have any idea what it means when a bird flies into your window?" he asked.

"It means the bird probably needs glasses," I joked.

He gave an obligatory laugh, then said, "I was serious. Do you know what it means?"

"Um . . . well . . . did it die?"

"No, no, it's not like that. It didn't happen just once. It's been happening over and over again, for days now. I hear it tapping at the window on the stairway landing, and when I go to look, there's this bird. It backs off with its wings flapping and it flies headfirst straight into the window. Then it does it again. And again. What do you think it means?"

I told him I had no idea. Frankly, I figured that either the bird was losing it—or maybe my father was.

A few days later we spoke again, and he told me it was still going on. "It starts in the morning," he said, uncharacteristically unsettled, "and it goes on all day. The same bird. Over and over."

I'll admit I thought he had to be exaggerating. Still, I did a bit of research online. I found out that, once in a while, a bird will mistake its reflection in a window as another bird in its territory and fly into the glass, usually injuring or even killing itself in the process. But for it to happen repeatedly, over a series of days? That was definitely far-fetched.

"Do you think it means anything?" my father asked me, and I knew what he was getting at.

He wanted to know if I thought there was anything paranormal about it. He tends to view me as the expert on that sort of thing, because I write books about it. And I tend to view him as a skeptic—though he's slowly coming around.

"I have no idea what it means," I told him, and we dropped the subject.

A few weeks later, I made the trip home with my family to celebrate my grandma's birthday. The first morning, I woke up in my childhood bedroom to a tapping sound. I got up and crept over to the top of the stairs . . . and sure enough, there at the window on the landing was a bird. It backed up, flapped its wings, and dive-bombed the window. Then it did it again. And again.

It went on all day.

"See?" my father said. "I told you. It's trying to tell me something."

We were all fascinated—my husband, my kids, my father, and I. But not my grandmother—my mom's mother. When she heard about it, she pretty much freaked. She's Sicilian, and superstitious, and apparently a bird hitting the window is not a happy omen.

I decided to call my friend Donna Riegel, who is a medium at Lily Dale. I told her I was in town and that something odd had been happening at my childhood home, but I didn't tell her what it was. She agreed to make a house call.

My sister, brother, and sister-in-law all wanted to be a part of Donna's visit, so six of us were there, including my father, my husband, and me. The bird had been doing its thing all day but was nowhere to be seen when Donna arrived. It was just as well, I decided. I wanted to see if she picked up on anything without such a blatant clue.

Donna felt my mother's energy the moment she walked in—a happy, positive energy. She spent the next few hours relaying messages from my mom. My husband, Mark, and I had seen Donna in action before, but even we were awed by how specific—and dead on—she was.

"You're going to be visiting the southwest," she informed my sister. "Not California . . . someplace closer. Texas? Are you going to Texas?"

My sister was, indeed, going to Texas. She and her family and my father had tickets to fly to Houston two days later.

Over and over, Donna told us things she couldn't have known—things my mother, however, would certainly have known. She mentioned an obscure song that was incredibly meaningful to my father, a letter hidden in the bottom of a drawer, and the fact that my brother—who is tall and lanky like the basketball player he once was—also played quarterback for the high school football team. Mom gave us—her three children—much-needed, specific advice. And she had loving words for my husband and my sister-in-law, both of whom she had adored.

Donna told my father that my mother strongly felt it was time for him to make some changes. She wanted him to move on and look ahead. She would always be with him, but he had a lot of living left to do. We were all comforted to hear that, knowing he had had a difficult road through the grieving process and that there were times he wished he didn't have to go on without her.

Though we had said something strange was going on, Donna didn't feel that it was negative energy, whatever it was. My father told her about the bird and asked what she thought it meant.

Donna was very honest. Basically she said, "It might just be a dumb bird . . . or it might be a message. I really couldn't tell you. Just pay attention, and if it's a message, you'll eventually find the meaning."

All of us were comforted by our mother's communications, regardless of whether we'd solved the mystery of the bird. We concluded that if the bird was my mother trying to tell my father something, then she was really, really frustrated that he wasn't getting it!

A strange thing happened after that day: the bird disappeared entirely.

Once Donna had come and gone, the bird stopped banging the window. No sign of it anywhere. We left town the next morning, and a couple days later, my father left to visit Texas with my sister. When he came home, late in April, he said the bird was still missing in action.

But by then, something was very wrong. My father wasn't feeling well. He thought he had the flu. When I visited him at the beginning of May, he was still very ill. My pop's an active guy in his sixties who loves to golf and travel and socialize. It takes a lot to get him even to call it a night. But there he was, lying down under a blanket in the middle of the afternoon with fever and chills.

We had planned for him to accompany me to Ohio on my book tour, and he insisted on going, as we'd planned. But when we got there, he was too sick to get out of bed at the hotel. I was alarmed.

I dragged him to a doctor, who told him he had a bacterial infection. "A few weeks on antibiotics," Pop told me as I flew home to my own life, "and I'll be good as new."

He wasn't. He didn't let on to any of us, but his health was declining rapidly. Finally, one morning, he couldn't get out of bed. My siblings called 911 and my father was rushed to the hospital with—it turned out—massive internal bleeding.

We were told he probably wouldn't have made it through another night in the house alone. As it was, he spent almost a week in the ICU. Now, weeks later, he's on the road to recovery.

After he was released from the hospital, he told me that, when he had lost consciousness, he had seen my mother. That's unusual because, unlike the rest of us, my father never, ever sees her in his dreams.

"I was in the living room, sitting in my chair," he said, "and she was there, too. She was sitting cross-legged in the air up over the couch. I asked her what she was doing there, and she just smiled and said she was with me, reading her book."

I have no doubt it meant that my mother was with him in the house through his long, frightening decline—and with him, too, in the terrifying touch-and-go days in the hospital.

It wasn't until much later that I remembered the bird. I reminded my father.

"I know," he said. "I've been thinking about it, too. I think it was a sign."

If the bird hadn't been there, we wouldn't have had Donna come over. My mother wouldn't have let my father know he still had a lot of living left to do. And maybe he wouldn't have fought so hard, and made it through.

The bird never did come back. And my father is doing just fine.